Coming Round the Mountain

'There's no way you're putting that thing up me!' I shouted.

'Shhh,' said the monk, his friends watching. 'We are experimenting with pleasure, to meet your desires, but that's all I can say. Remember the silence rule.'

One monk set about making things better, and another set to work, his tongue between my legs. It was fantastic. Too good to be true. Everything felt zingy and crazy and alive. A bizarre thought crossed my mind: The monk and the pussy. It struck me that this would be a good name for a pub.

D1638490

Other books by the author:

Tongue in Cheek
Full Steam Ahead
The Hottest Place

Coming Round the Mountain
Tabitha Flyte

BLACK LACE

Black Lace books contain sexual fantasies.
In real life, always practise safe sex.

First published in 2004 by
Black Lace
Thames Wharf Studios
Rainville Road
London W6 9HA

Copyright © Tabitha Flyte, 2004

The right of Tabitha Flyte to be identified as the Author of
the Work has been asserted by her in accordance with the Copyright,
Designs and Patents Act 1988.

Design by Smith & Gilmour, London
Printed and bound by Mackays of Chatham PLC

ISBN 0 352 33873 3

*All characters in this publication are fictitious and any resemblance
to real persons, living or dead, is purely coincidental.*

This book is sold subject to the condition that it shall not, by way
of trade or otherwise, be lent, resold, hired out or otherwise
circulated without the publisher's prior written consent in any form
of binding or cover other than that in which it is published and
without a similar condition including this condition being imposed
on the subsequent purchaser.

1

'I was told it was right here,' Stella said doubtfully, studying the serviette on which one of the boys at the hostel had drawn a map. It didn't look like a map, though; it looked more like a diagram one might find in a biology textbook.

'That can't be right,' I said confidently. We were outside an old building. The entrance was through a burnt wooden door at the bottom of some old stairs.

'There's no way that's a temple. Let me see . . .'

But Stella was more experienced in the ways of Nepal than me. She thumped down the steps and pushed at the door. Reluctantly I followed her inside.

We were faced with a long dark corridor, and by dark I mean pitch black. The air was moist and the walls were damp.

'I see a light,' I joked, but Stella put her fingers to her lips. 'Shh.'

I couldn't see anyone but I realised she meant that we weren't alone. I wanted to giggle or to shout for an echo to come back at us, but Stella was serious. She had wanted to see this place for a long time.

The corridor went on for longer than any corridor I'd walked down before. Finally, we were in a large dim room. I say large but it was large only in contrast with the corridor. It was, in fact, about the size of a double-decker bus.

'Oh wow,' I said when my eyes had become accustomed to the light. 'I don't believe this.'

Now it was Stella's turn for denial. 'This can't be right. It can't be.'

In the quiet, I could hear her swallow.

It was only my second day in Nepal. On my first I had taken a bus to Kathmandu city centre from the airport. I had sat next to a woman holding a chicken. The woman kept looking at me. The chicken looked out the window. I was tired. I'm not sure if I actually fell asleep, or if I just had a peculiar daydream. Whatever it was, when I groggily came around, all I could remember was the feeling that something momentous had happened, but I couldn't put my finger on what.

It was midnight by the time I got to the bus station, which meant it was way too late to turn back. Apart from the people who got off the bus, the chicken, and a few men in uniform lolling around smoking, the place was empty. I walked outside quickly, pretending that I knew what I was doing, and then I walked back inside. I didn't know what I was doing. I was terrified. After about ten minutes of this, another bus arrived and a Western woman got off. I didn't think twice about running over to her. I'm usually quite shy, so that shows how desperate I was. I introduced myself and said, 'Please, please do you know a good safe place I could go for the night?' The woman was Stella – who turned out to be alone too, although this was her eighth or ninth trip to Nepal. She knew a cheap hostel that did great breakfasts. She grinned at me before adding, 'I can't promise it'll be safe.' By then, though, I had cheered up completely. I thought, this is going to be OK.

Stella managed to hail a taxi. It was a dilapidated London Black Cab and we managed to arrive outside The Everest in five minutes flat. A single room was half the price of a twin, so we shared a bed. I didn't mind; I was that exhausted by then I could probably have slept standing in the street. From what I remember, she didn't snore too much although I don't think she would have said the same about me.

The next day Stella asked me if I wanted her to go out in the city with me.

'The first time can be quite an experience,' she explained. It wasn't until we had left the sanity of the hostel that I realised that she wasn't joking.

Buffalos wandered all over the streets. The motor-bikes could weave around them but the old cars and taxis just stopped and hooted their frustration. Buses pulled over to the sides of the road and the people sitting on their roofs waved and shouted things I couldn't understand, but something told me they were swear words.

I must have looked ridiculous. I was walking around a city that was more like an exploded village and most of the time my mouth hung open in surprise. It was all so incredible. I kept saying, 'This is so different from England,' and Stella kept saying, 'I know, I know. Isn't it mad?' The streets smelled of incense, dying flowers and burnt chicken. There were little shrines dotted here and there, and the people wore bright saris. I felt not like I had crossed to the other side of the world but that I had gone back in time. And yet, when I thought I had seen enough, there were more surprises. There were the stalls selling watermelons and singing bells. Some children gathered around for a spontaneous game of street football. There were elephants and donkeys and temple after temple after temple.

However, this temple, the one where we were at now, was by far the biggest surprise of all. It was so surprising that I actually forgot to try to shut my mouth at all.

You had to get up close to see that the engravings on the walls were of naked bodies and some depicted people having sex. There were intricate drawings and reliefs of hands, tongues, breasts, cunts and cocks on the ceiling. There were images of men being sucked off and women being licked out. They depicted sexual positions I didn't know existed. There were orgies, and 2 on 1s and 1 on 2s and 5-a-sides and goodness knows what else. Even the floor was replete with images of orifices; some were filled with fingers or tongues. Others were waiting, anticipating.

'Is this it?' I whispered. 'Is this what we were looking for?'

Stella didn't answer.

We walked into another room. There the walls were covered with gaps, some oval, some round, but all no longer than a finger. It was only after you put your finger in to touch the smooth carved-out surfaces that you realised they were intricately carved cunts and arseholes. Each was as individual as a thumbprint, and each was gaping, inviting the attention of probing fingers.

Here the ceiling scene showed two women together and two men together. I have seen pictures of Roman baths and Greek orgies, but they had nothing on these. There were engravings of women touching their breasts, and it seemed as if they were pushing them right at you, or had opened themselves out so you had no option but to look straight up them.

You would think, perhaps, that most of the visitors to this temple would be men. Yes, there were plenty of men there. They each had that glazed-eyed, biting-lip, stunned expression, but there were as many women with dreamy expressions as there were men. Later, I would find out that these scenes were commissioned to

4

excite men and women equally. At the time, though, I didn't know what they were except that they made me feel like I was missing something.

I watched one young girl with smooth black hair approach a wall. She pressed her breasts at a hole, and then leant against it. Her pretty face was puckered in ecstasy. She put her hands under her dress and moved her wrists up and down. Directly above her there was a picture of a man lying down and over him were loads of women all making love to each other in the 69 position. There was an engraving of a woman and a man. She was bent right over, and he was thrusting into her, but next to him there was a woman, a laughing woman, and she had one hand up his arse and her other up another woman's cunt.

I stood, almost dizzy. If these were real-life vaginas and arseholes, and they certainly seemed realistic enough, then who had modelled for them? Just what kind of person would want their genitals to be shown in a place like this?

I watched the young woman with the smooth black hair grab her breasts again, beneath her purple silk shirt, and rub them against the hole and then she was staring at something just behind me. She made this sound like a great 'Oh yeah', only it couldn't have been that; she wasn't speaking English, but it was something I guess that meant the same thing.

I turned to see what had caught her attention. It was a series of pictures of a woman. I think she was tied up, and she was surrounded by men in robes who were doing her in every way you can imagine – and some ways you couldn't. In the final picture, she was getting penetrated in just about every orifice. She had a cock in her pussy, one in her arse and one in her mouth, and she was being surrounded by a dozen more men waiting their turn. But you could tell from her face, even from a face relief in wood, that she wasn't uncomfortable; she was downright loving it.

The black-haired woman had good taste. It was mesmerising. I realised I was holding my breath. The hand that was on my stomach moved lower but uncertainly as though it belonged to someone else. I fiddled with the button of my jeans. I was so damp between the legs.

A guard rushed over.

'Ticket, please.'

Stella spoke. I had forgotten she was there. 'We don't have tickets but . . .'

I couldn't speak. The images were so sensual, but it wasn't just the images; it was the way everyone there was just slotting their fingers into the gaps and moving them along, around and up and down, engaging with the sculptures. I didn't trust myself to speak.

Out of the corner of my eye I saw a pale-faced man enter the room. He marched over to the far wall and then dropped to his knees. No matter that the floor was dirty with the footprints of so many visitors; what he was about to do was obviously more important than worrying about that. With an expression of great tenderness, he put his face to a hole. I watched his tongue emerge from between his lips and press to the hole. I saw him lick his way around it. He had both hands up against the wall to keep his balance. I couldn't help tucking my hand inside my T-shirt to touch my breasts, feeling warmth spread through me. The place was having an incredible influence on everyone, it seemed.

'You have to leave,' the guard commanded.

'No, we . . .'

The guard was joined by a woman wearing thick red lipstick. She looked furious.

'Please leave. Nationals only.'

'What does she mean?' I whispered to Stella.

'She means it's only for local people. We have to get out.'

They ushered us out a back door. Even as we protested they slammed it behind us. I wiped the hair off my forehead. I didn't know I had been sweating so much. Stella was perspiring too. She bit her lip and, although it wasn't her fault at all and there was nothing to apologise for anyway, she said, 'I'm so sorry, Lauren, I had no idea! That was disgusting, wasn't it?'

Disgusting? That wasn't exactly what I was thinking.

'Oh, yes,' I agreed, 'absolutely depraved. I can't believe people actually go there to . . . to . . . I don't know what.'

Later, safe in a café with an English menu, Stella asked me what I was doing in Kathmandu. She clearly didn't want to speak about our strange experience again. Stella was a project co-ordinator for a charity. She had a month off before she started working in India and she was just travelling around Nepal for a while. With her uneven features, she was more interesting-looking than attractive but in some lights, like here in this café, she was pretty in a once-you-get-to-know-her kind of way.

'I'm not doing anything much,' I said. 'I mean, I don't have an idea for a career path or anything.'

It was and wasn't true. I did feel that all my life I had been waiting to go somewhere, and as soon as I had stepped out of the plane on to that runway, I knew this was the place I was meant to be. When I was a child I had an encyclopedia and I used to spend hours gazing at pictures of mountains, imagining them alive. Each mountain had a different personality: Everest, of course, was the bossy one, but there were many others.

There were the hangers-on, the cheeky ones, the cute ones and the haughty ones. All this I deduced from their size and shape. I always had a thing for the cool, for the uninhabited. I loved the idea of a place where the stars were still the brightest thing at night.

I didn't tell Stella that, though. I thought Stella would think me odd. Perhaps she would think I wasn't 'goal-oriented' enough. That's what my mother said ever since she had taken a ten-week evening course in assertiveness. 'Lauren, if you want to get anywhere in life you have to have goals.' But I was disappointingly aimless while Stella had helped the poor and needy in Colombia, Mali, Ethiopia and a whole load of places I had never heard of. I didn't know about good works. Hell, I was poor and needy enough myself, thank you.

'I don't know if I could do what you do,' I admitted. I did admire her although I definitely wouldn't have wanted to have been like her. Last night, I saw that she didn't shave under her arms. The only make-up she wore was a lipstick so unsuitable she must have found it in a Christmas cracker.

'It's not that great.' For once Stella looked quite sad. 'It can be very lonely,' she said.

'Oh, I'm sure it isn't,' I gaily interjected. I didn't know her well enough to hear her heartaches. And I definitely wasn't ready to tell her mine. 'I suppose I just want to experience some stuff,' I said meekly. I felt more and more like I wasn't wise enough for this travelling lark. Who was I trying to kid? As for discovering myself, what was there to discover?

But Stella was kind. She said, 'You've come to the right place, Lauren. The sights here are out of this world.'

And we laughed and both conveniently managed not

to mention the temple we had seen, but I'm sure Stella hadn't forgotten it, and I knew I would never forget it either.

It wasn't until we were walking back to the hostel that evening that I saw the most amazing, and certainly the most unexpected, sight of all. Less than a foot in front of us stood a man so exceptionally good looking that he should have been preceded by a ticket office charging five dollars a peek.

He was tall, but not too tall, and not at all lanky. He was sturdy, quite wide across, all shoulders and chest, and he had the most beautiful face. He had heart-shaped lips, a row of sensual teeth and a perfect nose. He had dark blond hair and it was tousled superbly in the way that even people who usually prefer smooth hair (me!) would approve of.

And the thing was, I knew him. I knew him very well.

'Look, there,' I hissed to Stella.

'Oh yes, that's another famous temple,' Stella said. She smoothed out her map. 'Built in 1209, it's based on Chinese architecture and it suggests that there is an afterlife –'

'No, not that – him!' He was fiddling in his coat pockets for something. My heart, maybe. 'He's someone I used to know.'

Stella looked up, saw him and smiled knowingly at me. 'Is he? Are you going to say hello?'

Then I saw her. She was a bulky but healthy-looking girl in a fleece jacket, shorts and trainers. She too had dark blonde hair, but hers was scraped back into two bunches (not a good style, I must say, on the over-thirties, which she evidently was).

I would never have put them together. It was

nothing to do with her looks, which I suppose were on a par with his, but more the way that she looked. He was soft, not feminine, but inquiring and gentle. She was hard, hard and judgemental. I could tell. Maybe it was a yin-and-yang thing, maybe it was the age-old adage about opposites attracting, but from where I was standing it was almost an obscenity.

Perhaps it wasn't Callum. Maybe it was just someone who looked like him. For Christ's sake, it had been years. How would I know what he looked like now?

I looked at the man's arms. Callum had always had the most distinctive arms. More hairy than a woman's but not too hairy, dark brown and with a shape that told you exactly how fit he was.

Yes, it was definitely him.

The woman went into a shop. He waited outside. And I thought, yes! Maybe they were together only in the way travellers hook up, like Stella and me. Travellers can't be choosers; anyone who shares a language or has the same colour passport is a potential friend.

Eventually he saw me gawping at him. I saw the change that came over him as he realised who I was. I saw him frame my name with his lips first before the sound came out.

'Lauren, is that you?'

Even if he hadn't said my name I would have known from his voice that it was him. His voice was just the same as it was back then. It was perfectly pitched, steady. It was a voice made for comfort – 'Everything is going to be just dandy' – or command – 'Take your knickers off' – according to his mood.

And then we were hugging and slapping each other on the back.

'Callum, I can't believe it's you! What the fuck are you doing here?'

Callum gently shoved me back in order to take a look at me. 'You look like an ice princess.'

'And you, Callum, you look so well.'

I can't remember what else was said for I was too caught up watching his body and wondering what it would feel like against my skin again. I was asking questions but not listening to the answers. I was just listening to his voice pour over me the way it used to. As we stood there some kids bolted by, chasing a football, and he grabbed my arm to stop them careening into me. Waves of excitement rushed through me. It was still there, all of it: all the old emotions, all the old tensions. Nothing had disappeared, but instead of feeling happy or relieved, or I don't know ... I just felt terrified.

If he had wanted to kiss me there and then, I would have agreed. No, who am I kidding? If he had wanted to fuck me there and then, I would have jumped at the chance. He was far better looking than he used to be, and he was good looking then.

The woman emerged from the shop holding a brown paper bag. I stared at Callum, challenging him, I suppose, and he hesitated. The woman didn't seem too pleased to see him with us.

'The people here are so damn slow. I wanted a stamp and it took them ages to realise what I was asking for,' she moaned.

'Why should they?' I said. My first impressions of Callum's friend were not all together positive. 'English is not their native language,' I continued.

She looked at me as though I was arguing that the world was flat and she should walk off it.

'They should,' she replied, 'because this is a tourist area. They have to serve people well, otherwise they won't get any more custom.'

'Well, maybe they don't wa –'

'These two are from England,' Callum spoke up.

The girl looked at us for a few seconds – long enough to show that it was only for his sake that she would lower herself to talk to us.

'Hi! English people!' She stuck out a pink hand; I had a vision of a pig's trotter. 'I'm Chelle, and this, I'm sure you've forgotten to introduce yourself – you're such a nit sometimes – is Callum.'

The words swivelled around my head. *'You're such a nit sometimes'*? What was that all about?

'What are your names then?' she asked.

I stared at Callum's feet in their leather sandals. He still had slim legs, but he was much heavier upstairs. Of course, when I knew him he was still more boy than man (physically, I mean, not mentally). Now he was all man. He was the sort who, when he held you, made you feel safe. You knew that if you were in some disaster movie, this would be the guy to rescue you from the collapsing ceiling. He was the guy who not only would save you from the attentions of the baddie but would also give you the best seeing-to of your life in the elevator as it plummeted 600 metres. But it was his face that really did it for me, I must admit. Then and now. More now maybe than back then even. Such cheekbones, such eyebrows. But Callum wasn't just a great body or even pretty face. He was an artist. He made things. Sometimes he worked with wood, sometimes with clay. He painted pictures that made you think. You could tell he was an artist from his hands.

I looked at his hands and I wanted his hands on me then. I wanted to kiss him or gobble him up whole. Now that we were close, I hardly dared look at him. But he smiled at me and, for a split second, he was between my legs, his face stained with my juices, and he was diving down between my thighs, nuzzling my pussy. I had to shake myself away from the thoughts. I remembered his cock, his eighteen-year-old cock, straight as an arrow and firm as a peach. I almost sighed aloud.

'Lauren,' he said and I couldn't think of anything to say. Bizarrely, all I could think of doing was flashing him my tits – which I didn't. I waited for him to tell her, to tell her who I was, and who I had been to him, but he didn't say anything.

He still likes me, I decided. Maybe Chelle had followed him and he couldn't shake her off. I wondered how we could get rid of her. I could say that I had forgotten something at the hostel; he could accompany me back. His eyes shining on me gave me confidence. I hadn't had sex in a very long time.

It was when Stella started to talk about her job that Chelle decided we passed muster. Yes, she would lower herself to talk to the peasants.

'You are going to actually work in India? Fantastic! Wonderful!' Chelle banged on, asking questions only to interrupt Stella's admittedly rather laborious answers. 'They so need people like you to sort this country out. My goodness, I knew it was poor in Nepal but I had no idea!'

Callum and I stood side by side. I liked to think it was as though we were allied against the idiots. Chelle must have decided that Stella's tale was not sensational enough for now she interrupted her with talk about the mountains, about never getting an opportunity like this again, about yoga, her special diet, about persuading her boss for one month's holiday, paid of course, and the very unique pressures of having a high-powered job, and so on.

'So, how come you are in Nepal?' I whispered to Callum. He and Chelle could be part of a group, maybe they were co-workers, or perhaps they belonged to the same stupid yoga club. *Who would call their boyfriend a nit?* 'And how come you're with ... er ... Chelle?' I had to conceal my chuckles. She was so the kind of girl we would have laughed at once: arrogant, earnest and completely, utterly sexless.

I couldn't resist smiling up at him, meeting his eyes with unspeakable promises. They couldn't be boyfriend and girlfriend, I told myself. No fucking way.

I was right.

'Me and Chelle are on honeymoon,' he said.

That night was the worst and the best in my memory. Stella had looked so crestfallen when I said I was going back and, although I hadn't known her for long, I didn't want to annoy her. Still, although I pretended to myself that it was for Stella's sake that I stayed, that wasn't the whole truth. I didn't particularly want to spend any more time with them, any of them, but I couldn't bare the thought of leaving them either.

I was absolutely smitten. All over again.

We ate dinner on the flat roof of a restaurant on the other side of the city. Chelle claimed it wasn't very touristy but the only customers there were Westerners like us. Still, it was a balmy evening and the stars seemed to blink down at us benevolently.

'The sky is so much more beautiful here than at home,' said Chelle. I was annoyed because that was exactly what I was thinking and I didn't like the idea that she and I were thinking the same thing although, as far as Callum was concerned, I have no doubts that our thoughts were not only identical but Siamese in nature. (Oh, if only he and I were joined at the hip!)

Callum was the same as he used to be but older, of course. He was always confident, but now that confidence seemed genuine, or at least earned. Where once he had been cocky, he was quieter; he was less inclined to interrupt or even offer his opinion, but maybe that was because of her.

What would it be like to kiss him again?

I learned that they lived near Chelle's family. They had met each other at work. Chelle used to be Callum's boss. It seemed to me that she still was.

'What work do you do now, then?'

'We both work in insurance,' Chelle said. She didn't let him answer anything.

I was so shocked. 'Insurance? Worrying about things that might never happen, eh?'

'Yes, but they might,' Callum said.

I tried to raise my eyebrows at him, to turn it into something sexy but he was looking away.

'Insurance is a great field to be in right now,' Chelle said, as though she was talking to a new office junior. 'Reliability; that's what you want from your job.'

I remembered the things Callum used to say about reliable jobs; about reliable cars; all for people with limited imaginations. How could he have changed so? Had he become one of the people who couldn't imagine anything different?

Then he grinned up at me and I realised he hadn't changed.

The tables were small and Callum's legs were long. We banged knees and, every time his leg touched against mine, I had to draw in breath for my heart was beating so strongly. He was next to her, though, and sometimes their hands disappeared for what felt like forever.

When the main course came, to accommodate his long legs I opened mine. His leg pressed against my inner thigh. It was a pleasing arrangement. Heat radiated from my knees and I wrapped my thighs around him. I felt like my leg was swelling, expanding, just to be near him.

I tried not to think of the sights I had seen in the day. I tried not to think of the temple, especially the scene of the woman tied down by all the men. I mean, that didn't appeal to me at all, no way, not on any level, but the more I told myself not to think about it, the more I couldn't help it. Was that woman with the smooth black hair masturbating to it? What would I have done if we had stayed there for longer?

I was soaking wet between my legs.

I didn't speak much, but then I didn't have to. Chelle rattled on enough for all of us. Occasionally she would look to Callum for agreement and he would nod enthusiastically, though I didn't know if he was keeping up with her any better than I was.

I wanted his knee to go further up. I wanted him to press me between my legs. Let me ride on him. I wanted him to fuck me. It was hard to concentrate on anything else. I had forgotten what that feeling of horniness felt like; how close to desperation it was. It was pretty nice to remember it again. So I wasn't *completely* past it.

Stella seemed quite taken by Chelle. When Chelle went to the loo, Stella whispered to me, 'Chelle's quite interesting. I know that what she said about the people annoyed you but . . .'

'That's not all that annoyed me,' I said jealously, and Stella gave me a look.

On the way back, Chelle and Stella marched ahead, while Callum walked alongside me. I held back deliberately. I even pretended I had a limp for a moment to slow us down until I saw that Callum was looking at me strangely.

I was imagining that it was the two of us who were

married and *we* were on the honeymoon. It didn't seem that odd. We intimately inhaled the same air; it came out of his mouth and into mine. I pretended that Chelle and Stella no longer existed.

I suppose I would have managed this better if he hadn't started talking about Chelle and about what a great trip this was going to be and...

'So how come you married?' I interrupted. 'You never seemed the marrying kind.'

I had to know. It was hurting already. At least Callum didn't look surprised or offended, though his answer, to my mind, was less than satisfactory.

'We've been together seven years, and I thought, I'm never going to meet anyone else, I mean, anyone better than her.'

Everyone is better than her, I thought. *Even I am better than her and you never...*

'I suppose that's why most people do.'

'Do what?'

'Get married,' he repeated. 'That's what you asked, isn't it?'

One moment Chelle and Stella were ahead of us, the next there were only old men with Biblical beards and women rushing home with bags of fruit. We turned another street corner and there was no one around. I smelled hay, wet straw or something. We had lost them and we had lost our way too. Could he insure against that?

'I'm afraid,' I said, although I wasn't.

'Don't worry, I'm with you.' I could tell from his voice that he was smiling.

'That's what I'm afraid of.'

I wondered if he knew how close he had come to masturbating me with his knee in the restaurant. *Callum, do you remember? Do you remember me?*

He took my hand and my body rushed out, every fibre, every nerve, every part of me rushed towards him, pleading for him to touch me.

'You're shaking.' He covered my hand. 'There's nothing to worry about.'

'Isn't there?'

He must have felt it too. There was still so much between us. I felt like I was under a magic spell. I was melting. My whole body was liquid. I couldn't look at him. I wanted to press myself against him. I wanted to feel his cock grow hard against my thigh. I wanted to hold him there, rub him up and down and, when he was ready, put it in me, take it inside me, feel it pump inside me. It was that bad; a sliver of wetness actually ran down my leg.

'Callum,' I said, 'I can't believe we found each other again.'

I took his hand and held it tight. Our hands fitted together perfectly. I mean, we even knew which finger to put between which. It was *so* sexy.

He cleared his throat. 'Oh, Lauren, I feel –'

'Oi, over here!' Under a streetlamp Stella and Chelle were circled by a halo of gold light. Callum and I were still in the darkness.

'There you are,' barked Chelle. She stomped over to us and took Callum's arm. 'What's the matter with you tonight?'

'I was just saying I've known Lauren –' he paused '– and Stella for ages. It feels like that, at least.'

'That's travelling for you,' said Chelle. God, I hated her. 'You get to know people so quickly.'

We walked back to the hostels silently. It was so cold we could see our breath come out of our mouths. It seemed even Chelle had run out of things to complain about.

As we parted, Callum leaned forward and kissed me on the cheek. I was unprepared and I tilted my head ever so slightly, but the result was that his lips fell on the corner of my mouth.

'Night, Callum.' Oh, I was so casual. I was good.

'Night night, babes,' he said. He was a dragon, breathing fire into me.

And then Chelle kissed the mountain air next to my cheek, and I obediently pecked the air next to hers.

2

I had met Callum sixteen years earlier. It was a warm, muzzy July. Frankie Goes to Hollywood and Chaka Khan was the soundtrack to my world.

Callum had just left school and was working as a deckchair attendant on the Margate promenade while he prepared a portfolio for art college. He marched up and down the sand squinting in the sunlight. He wore shorts with a money bag slung low around his slim hips. He was tall and brown. He was the sort of boy who would have nothing to do with me. I wasn't a summer girl; I wasn't a beach girl at all. When people looked at me, they said, 'Wrap up warm', or, 'It must be cold out there.'

That's why I was at home in Nepal, I suppose. I had the mountains in my blood. Without even knowing it, I yearned for lush valleys, green mountains with white snow caps, and small teahouses in the middle of nowhere. But he, Callum, my summer boy, was in my blood too.

I had just done my exams. They were O levels back then, and I was to start sixth form that September. I was ready for something, but at the time I didn't know what.

The first thing he ever said to me was, 'Are you going to come in the water?'

I hated swimming. I much preferred a pair of heavy boots and a grey rock face, even then. I said, 'I'm not getting in there.'

'Suit yourself,' he said but he didn't move away. I could see droplets of sweat on his legs. No drops of sweat ever held my attention like they did. I wanted to touch them. I sat there, clasping sand only to have it run through my fingers, and I was thinking, what would his sweat actually taste like?

'You're missing out.'

'I'll live with it.'

'You know, you're pretty...'

'Yeah?' I was used to the old joke: pretty ugly, pretty sad. But he didn't add anything else. He just gazed at me, and I knew he was asking more than if I would be getting in the water with him.

Of course, I did get in, in the end. And when he asked if I would be coming back, I said yes. I would always say yes. Callum was the kind of guy you didn't say no to, back then at least.

Now Stella and I got the key from reception. The receptionist was a young skinny bloke with narrow shoulders and an equally thin moustache. He was listening to music on his headphones and didn't notice us at first. When he did, he walked over with a huge smile.

'Oasis. English band, you like?'

'Sure,' I said. It made a change from the usual small talk about football.

'Tea for you, ladies?'

We said no thank you. I added that I was dog-tired. 'All we want to do is go to bed.'

'Ah, bed, yes,' he said winking at us. 'The English ladies all sleep together.'

He pushed the key in my palm. His hand was surprisingly warm.

As we left, I said to Stella, 'Did he think we were lesbians?'

'No, why? Why should he?' Stella looked concerned.

'I was only joking,' I said. *Jeezus!* 'Who cares what he thinks anyway? He can think what he likes.'

Stella frowned. It seemed she was about to say something but she didn't. For the first time I wondered if going halves on the room with her was such a good idea if she got so upset by a little comment like that! And the way she had reacted about that temple today. Anyone would think she was thirteen, not the cold side of thirty-five.

'As long as *you* don't mind,' she said finally.

The corridors of the hostel were pitch black. Everything seemed threatening at night. I knew Stella was nervous too and she was probably feeling slightly guilty. After all, she was the one who had recommended this place. The lights were on a saving device – you had to press a light and run to the next floor and put that light on too. Stella had a slim pen torch but she had left it on the bedside table in the room. While we were galloping between third and fourth, Stella asked, 'So, do you still feel anything for Callum now?'

'Oh no, that's all done and dead and buried. It was all a long, long time ago.' I found the button. Light flooded the corridor and made everything look quite different.

Now I felt silly that I had been so afraid.

'You two can go off on your own while Stella and I do some proper sightseeing.'

The next morning, Chelle was wearing a T-shirt that said 'Sexy little piggy'. She had on long brown shorts, for heaven's sake, orange, very expensive-looking trainers and a fluffy sleeveless jacket. Her hair was scraped back into the one ponytail this time. She had broad symmetrical features but I saw with more than a little satisfaction that, unlike me, she had a flat chest. Mine had really grown since I was a teenager. I was a late developer but my knockers were now my best feature.

Chelle was so bossy too. She was standing there with her guidebooks, her camera round her neck, telling us what to do.

'I think it will be better if we separate because Stella and I just *have* to see the Stupa.'

'The Stupa?' I giggled.

'That's right.' She looked at me coolly. 'And if we separate, we will all get to see what we want to see. You and Callum don't know what the hell you want to do anyway.'

'I don't know about that,' Callum said. He went behind Chelle and nuzzled her neck. He didn't look at me. 'I don't want to leave you, babe. It's dangerous; strange place, strange city, strange men . . .'

'That sounds like a good thing to me!' She winked at me conspiratorially. 'Oh no, I keep forgetting I'm on honeymoon!'

Chelle gave Callum a final lingering (or was it a malingering?) kiss.

'Go on. Go with Lauren to the river or wherever it is you two lazy-bones want to hang out. I'll see you back at the hostel at six.'

Needless to say I was thrilled by this turn of events. At last some time with Callum, alone! But my euphoria rapidly wore off as Callum was behaving really coolly towards me. Not only that, but I realised how inept we were in this strange city without our leaders. Unlike Chelle and Stella, we had only vague ideas of what we wanted to see. Chelle was right; neither of us had a clue.

Eventually Callum shook off the despair Chelle's absence seemed to have set in him. He jumped to his feet and he even managed to hail us a rickshaw. He climbed in first and I lumbered up next to him. I watched our legs rub, rub, rub against each other. He was wearing jeans, and I think they were done up by buttons, not zip. I imagined slipping my fingers there to his crotch and unbuttoning him slowly. I would pull his prick out from his pants. He would be hard. I could duck down and take him in my mouth. The thought of the groan he would make almost made me do it, but I didn't. I looked away. I could have moved further to the side of the rickshaw, but I kept to the middle, close to him. I wanted to see how he would react. But he didn't give anything away.

The driver wanted to know where we were going. He jiggled around impatiently. I remembered that we should have agreed a price before we got in and I worried that we were about to be stitched up. What a start that would be . . .

'The river then?' Callum suggested hesitantly, and the driver nodded like it was a great choice. I liked that idea too. I thought the two of us might hold each other, clasp each other, and do it by the shimmering blue light of the river, with the water lapping at our toes. I wondered if Callum remembered all the things he used to tell me, all those things about light and shade and shadows. Sometimes he did sketches of the people he had seen on the beach. I collected all the pictures he didn't want and I stuck them all over my room. Until the day I burned them one by one on the hob. How quickly the ladies in bikinis and the children licking ice creams, which my Callum had created, dissolved.

'You haven't told Chelle, have you?' I asked.

'Told her what?'

'About us.' I didn't think we had dissolved so quickly.

'Us?'

'About ... who I was.'

'What's there to tell?' Callum said. 'I mean, really, it was so long ago.'

Well, that put me firmly in my place. I couldn't bring myself to say any more. I wondered what Callum would do if I showed him that temple Stella and I had discovered. Maybe that would remind him of what we once were. But his words had thrown my experiences up in the air. I didn't know what he thought of me, what he thought about the sex we had back then. Maybe I had made a mistake. Maybe we never were in love. Had any of it happened anyway?

The river wasn't what I expected either. For a start, the colour was all wrong; it was brown, not blue, and it was surrounded by stone walls. There wasn't a grassy bank to be seen. There were no places to canoodle, no places to get back on to memory lane and, actually, even if we had found the ideal spot, the cold would have prevented us. An arctic wind whipped our faces and hands. I thought of Chelle in her silly shorts and I had to laugh.

We walked alongside the river. We didn't say much. Later we stretched out for the picnic. I was wearing a long dress because I remembered Callum used to like me in skirts. Or did he? I was beginning to be confused. Maybe I had imagined everything. On the steps nearby, among the traders selling fruits, necklaces and rings, a naked man with dreads smoked roll-ups. It made me want to giggle.

'That's a sadhu,' Callum said after a while. It seemed we were both looking for things to say.

'A sad-do?'

'They believe that by experiencing pain they can eliminate desire and therefore no longer suffer.'

'I don't get it. So, if they have loads of suffering, they can, kind of, not suffer?'

'I'm not sure,' he admitted. 'I think the point is if you don't desire, you don't suffer.'

I desired Callum, and I was suffering, but I suppose it wasn't a terrible kind of suffering. I mean it felt pretty good. In a way it was reminding me that I was alive.

I lay on the bank and thought how it would be if Callum just rolled on top of me. I could clasp his buttocks and pull him deep into me. I would bring my feet up to his back, keep him in so tight, jerk my pelvis up and down, and make him kiss me deep low down there.

I looked over at him and saw that he had his eyes shut. I was just about to lean over and touch his stomach but he must have felt my shadow because he opened his eyes and lifted himself up. He started awkwardly.

'I was going to tell Chelle about you, but I changed my mind.'

'Why?'

'She might get jealous.'

'Oh,' I said innocently. 'Is she the jealous kind?' I hoped she was. I hoped she would be revealed to be a wicked harridan who never let him have any fun.

'No.'

'Oh?' Why else would she be jealous then, I wondered, unless, that is, he still felt something for me?

Callum took a bite of flat bread. He munched for ages before he replied. 'Yeah, you're right. I shouldn't worry. Our relationship is pretty strong, you know, and sex with her is just breathtaking.'

'Oh really?' I put down my naan. I suddenly didn't like the taste. 'How's that?'

'It is, when you love someone.'

'You say that like you think I wouldn't know.'

'I don't know. I didn't mean it to sound that way. I just don't know you now.'

I'm the same person as I was, I wanted to shout. It's you who has changed.

Back then, when I was sixteen and he was eighteen, we never had trouble finding things to talk about. Callum said we connected on 'every level'. He said he had never expected to find someone he would feel so close to. We didn't have sex straight away though. Callum and I held out all July and August. There was a song around at that time that I took for our song: 'We don't have to take our clothes off, to have a good time.'

I don't know if Callum agreed with the lyrics, but he went along with them. Now, of course, I wonder: Callum wasn't a virgin when I met him, not like I was. Of course, there was the Rose Connelly thing, but even before all that unravelled there was O'Harts. O'Harts bar was run by a band of crazy Irish brothers, and it was the best bar in town – at least, it was the best for under-age drinking. Callum used to go there every Friday and Saturday night. He said it was for the atmosphere but, looking back, maybe it was because there was a barmaid there who slept with everyone, like it was included in the cost of the drink.

Anyway, I met him at the beach every day that summer, even though the beach wasn't my natural habitat. Callum laughed when I told him that.

'Yeah, you'd be more at home in the mountains, wouldn't you?' he'd said.

The truth was that for him I would have *moved* mountains. I watched him stride up and down the sand, looking for people sitting on his deckchairs. When he found them, they had to pay him 50p. Nobody seemed to mind though. Callum was like a ray of sunlight. Everyone who met him liked him. And I would watch him, shivering, pressing my legs together and thinking, later, later. For the moment he was public. Later, he would be mine. Later, he would bend me backwards on to his bed. Later he would kiss my throat and put his hands on my flanks. And it didn't bother me much that he charmed the customers. Well, I was only bothered by the very pretty ones, because he didn't give me cause to be concerned. He liked me best of all. At least, that's what he said.

At the seafront kiosk, they dipped flour mixture into the boiling oil and pulled out donuts, deep-fried and perfect, glistening with the white dusting sugar. I always bought two donuts and, without asking, they put them in two bags – a donut for me and a donut for him. Both for later, later. After we had rolled and rubbed, and after he came in my hand or in my mouth or on my face, we would open the paper bags and take out our prizes.

Sometimes, as I sat on the beach in my cardigans and warm clothes, I couldn't help but cup my breasts thinking of him.

We didn't take our clothes off, but we played around.

We met at a car park just off the beach after six. If he got there before me, he would get off his motorbike, take off his helmet and lean against the wall, so that I didn't know how long he had been waiting, but it looked like a long, long time. I liked to get there first. I liked the way he looked, straddling the motorbike, driving up for me. If I got there first I would climb on the bike before I said hello. We would go vroom, vroom, and I would play with his belt strap. I loved it. I loved pretending I was a sunny rock chick when, in reality, I was the snow queen.

The first time I got on the bike I collapsed over the side. I went straight over – thwack! Callum laughed like the world was ending. The second time I got on firm on the saddle and he kissed me on the lips and said, 'That's my girl.'

We rode around town. I thought everyone was looking at me. I *wanted* everyone to look at me. How I pitied everyone in their boring reliable cars. We, by contrast, were close to nature; the wind was on our bodies and the sun was on our cheeks. 'Born to be wild,' I said. 'Born to be together,' he said. We went back to his house and, if his family was out, we had the rule of the place. Each room served as our bedroom. We were masters of foreplay; we came all over the house. His cock was never out of my mouth and his fingers dipped into me. In and out, he went, out and in. 'Suck me, babe,' he said. 'Oh yeah, just like that.'

We had a good time.

Sometimes he would get up and draw the things he had seen at the beach. He was still experimenting with style, he said. I told him he could experiment with me any time. I liked his charcoal work best. The black lines on white paper spoke directly to me. He didn't. He always said they needed something else. Sometimes he would use spray paints in gold or silver. The sea looked good like that. He painted nearly anything but he never painted me. He claimed it would be impossible to capture me on paper. I never knew whether to take that as a compliment or not.

After we split, of course, I decided that it wasn't.

He was a happy guy. He was an optimist. The only thing he didn't like was not having any money. 'Get used to it,' I told him. 'That's the artist's life.' It didn't bother me at all. I planned to find a good job to support him. I wouldn't mind working in some office if it had strong air conditioning and pictures of my mountains on the walls. That would be enough for me, I told him, if I could be with him always.

Sometimes I thought he would go off me, find me gloomy, cloudy or morose, but he never did; at least he never *said* he did. I suppose though, in the end, he must have.

That evening, Stella and I ate in the hostel restaurant. It was a cool, uninviting room but the food was cheap. On the TV over our table they played Bollywood movies. I watched the men and women come together, pull apart, come together again, and pull apart again, as if they were attached to elastic bands. I didn't understand the words but the story was a doddle: they were in love, there were obstacles, but love overcame those obstacles. And then everybody danced.

There were no other customers in the restaurant, and that made me self-conscious. I wanted to leave as soon as we had eaten but Stella chatted happily and pondered whether to have coffee or not. 'What a place Nepal is! There is something unexpected around every corner,' she said. She would 'never get to grips with it'. Like the mountains that dissected it, Nepal was impenetrable. Apparently, Stella and Chelle had come across a festival and they had got their arms hennaed, look, and they had plaited their hair and everything was amazing. She said that Chelle loved the Stupa. Then Stella asked me how my day with Callum was, but I didn't know what to say. She seemed to want me to tell her something, to explain something, but I couldn't.

'Callum is pretty impenetrable too, you know,' I said, and, because I wanted her to think that I was joking and that I didn't care, I winked.

'And Chelle's not as horrible as you think,' Stella said, and then she looked embarrassed.

'What do you mean?' I really did want to know because I had to find out what Callum saw in Chelle. I guessed she must have been really good at sex – because she wasn't sweet, she wasn't beautiful, and she definitely wasn't as smart as she thought she was.

'I just mean . . .' Stella was about to say something and then she changed her mind. 'She wanted to go to the temple. You remember? The one we saw yesterday?'

Oh yes, I remembered.

'You didn't take her there though?' I asked. It was somehow very important to me that Chelle hadn't been.

'No, no, I mean, yuk! I wouldn't go back there, not if you paid me.'

'Right.' I knew I sounded unconvinced, so I added, 'Urgh. Let's forget about the coffee, yeah?'

Back in our room we both got in the bed and lay down stiffly. You know when someone gets in a toilet cubicle next to you and you want the other person to pee first? Well, I felt like that then, only I was desperate for Stella to fall asleep before I did. I really did. It was just that I knew I would feel more comfortable that way. Eventually, and it felt like a long old wait, Stella's breathing changed. I presumed she was asleep, leaving me to relax with my own thoughts. My thoughts turned to the temple. It was the face of the tied-up woman that stayed with me. The artist had perfectly caught the look of troubled ecstasy, the helplessness and yet the joy of her features as the men came at her. I visualised their cocks in her face, in her pussy, in her arse. That must hurt, I thought. It wasn't possible anyway, and who would want that? Stella was right – yuk.

And then I thought about Callum. I imagined his hands were on me. I imagined his hands were pulling my breasts tight and pinching my nipples taut. I wondered if Callum was lying with Chelle now, doing that to her yet thinking of me – and hating himself for it. I imagined him fucking her and dreaming of me, exploring her pussy, yet thinking of mine. I pictured him going lower, lower, kissing her belly but wishing he was doing the same to me. I thought about him inserting a little finger into her, putting his fingers in Chelle, but thinking of me. I put my hand down over my stomach. I travelled down to the mound of pubic hair. Was Callum doing the same to her? Was he wishing he was fucking me? Her pubic hair would be fairer than mine, and perhaps curlier. He would run his fingers through her pubes and then travel up her cunt, until she moaned and started to rock into him. I rolled on to my stomach.

Next to me, Stella gave out a little groan of restlessness and clasped her pillow. I knew I had to be quiet. I kissed my arm. I was passionate. I wrapped my lips around my skin, wishing it were him. It was him. His lips, his tongue was inside me. Callum, hurry Callum, feel me, and feel my wetness. Please touch my cunt. I parted my legs further. Was he doing that to her? Was he finding his way inside her? Was he amazed at her wetness like he would be amazed at mine? I will show him I can open my legs wider than she can. I can groan louder than she can. I am wetter than she is.

I didn't plan to masturbate with Stella right next to me. But once I started, her presence didn't seem such a hindrance. In fact, it kind of added to the situation. She lay there oblivious, little wisps of breath audible, little sighs coming out of her sweet open mouth. She had no idea.

Did Callum wonder about me? Did he wonder how I'd react? Did he imagine himself in bed with me? Didn't he want to know if I had changed in all these years or if I came in the same way?

Callum, I promised, for you, I will throw my arms away from my body. I will writhe on the mattress. I will whisper your name between deep sighs, deep animal sighs. I will drive you crazy with desire. Yes, Callum, you can fuck her as long as you think of me. I'll show you how I come. If you compare her to me, I will win every time.

I needed something inside. I was soaking wet and desperate. My fingers weren't enough. Stella slept innocently. What would she do if she discovered me? Maybe she was doing the same now. I turned on to my back and spread my legs wider under the sheets. All the time I had to be careful not to touch her. I got her pocket pen-light off the table and slid it between my thighs. It was smooth but bumpy and it went right in. I pulled it out and then in, just to feel the pleasure of it going out and in again and again. Oh yes, this was Callum's dick and Callum was fucking me. I was dribbling, biting the pillow. I had to be quiet. I could do that but I couldn't stop.

'Callum, I love you,' I whispered. 'And I'm going to have you and you're going to love it.' I realised that I might not be as aimless as I had thought. In fact, you could say, I was becoming quite goal-oriented. I worked the torch up and down me and thought what Callum would say if he could see me now … if only he could have been here.

Beside me, Stella snorted in her sleep.

3

The next evening Stella came back with some news. It seemed Chelle and Callum had booked a walking trip. It was right near the end of the season – soon it would be too cold to go up into the mountains – but they had managed to secure one of the very last guided walks.

'It's much cheaper to go trekking as a group,' Stella explained. The other guys who were due to go with them apparently were great, real experienced walkers. Unfortunately, they weren't experienced enough to avoid getting sick; they had both succumbed to the nightmare Delhi belly and had taken to their beds. Callum and Chelle thought they would have to cancel. Then they had had a better idea: why didn't Stella and I go with them instead?

'I don't get it,' I said to Stella. 'Why do they want us to come?'

Was it Callum? I really wanted to ask. Did Callum want me to come? Had he arranged it to be like this?

'Well . . .' Stella hesitated. I could see she was hunting for the right words. 'I think they wanted me to come and I explained you were on your own and I wouldn't leave you, so . . . so in the end they invited both of us.'

'Oh.' Stella politely looked at her hands and I wished I hadn't asked. 'So how are Chelle and Callum anyway? I assume you met up with them today.'

'Fine.' Sometimes Stella wasn't the most effusive. Today she was wearing a bizarre outfit. Round her neck she had tied something, only it wasn't a scarf. It appeared to be a flowery tablecloth and it clashed terribly with her stripy top.

'Getting on well?'

Stella laughed. She could make me feel like a dork sometimes. 'Most people on honeymoon do, don't they?'

Now it was my turn to laugh.

Anyway, the question was, was I willing to do the trek? I was here to go trekking anyway but I had planned a trip to a monastery first. I had just been reading about a very special place where you could learn to eliminate your desires in order to end your suffering. The guidebook devoted pages to the monastery's quiet, its atmosphere of self-discovery. I thought I might learn to meditate there. I suppose I hoped to come away a calmer, wiser person.

It was that or spend time with Callum.

I didn't take long to decide.

The monastery could wait.

Still I hesitated a little more to make Stella sweat. She was dying to go with them on the trek and I could tell she was regretting having insisted I went along too. After all, we hardly knew each other. I don't know if I would have done the same for her.

'So you think it will be good, this trek?'

'Oh yes,' she said. 'It's not so much a trek as a great big walk really.'

'I suppose I could go to the monastery later,' I said like it was a great sacrifice.

'So, shall I tell them yes?'

'I don't care,' I said. 'Oh, if you really want, why not?'

Yes. God, yes. I couldn't wait to see Callum again. And to see Callum up in the mountains, watching the sunrise and the sunset with his cock thrusting inside me? Well, that would be something else . . .

* * *

On the last day of that long summer holiday, sixteen years ago, Callum and I were at the beach, as we were the first day. Callum walked along looking fine, as usual taking money for the chairs. He came over for a kiss and a chat. He always found me; he always knew where I was, even though I was never in the same place. My friends liked moving around. My friends wanted to meet boys although when we did meet any, my friends ignored them. But what did I care? I had Callum. I knew Callum was the best guy in the town; the best guy in the world maybe. Sometimes my friends tried to make me feel bad for being so happy, so settled, so young! But it didn't work. They all wanted Callum. They didn't say they did but their eyes said it for them. They watched every move we made. They licked their ice creams like they wished they were licking him. But Callum ignored them. He had eyes only for me. And that's what made him even more appealing, I suppose.

I did wonder why he liked me. I was the palest girl of the bunch. I didn't go topless. Back then, what would have been the point? Anyway, Callum said he liked to know there was something to uncover. He didn't like to be offered it all on a plate. He said you need some mystery otherwise you know everything before you've even started. I disagreed. I mean, sex is not some kind of detective story; if you need mystery maybe that's because you haven't got something else.

Until that day, we had been kissing and touching, licking and sucking, but I didn't expect anything else to happen. We were happy like that. You know, dieters say they start losing weight very quickly at first and then they reach a kind of plateau. Well, we had hurried through our stages, fingering, blow-jobs and so on, and then we too had reached a plateau. It wasn't a problem though, this plateau. We were quite civilised. 'We aren't animals,' Callum used to say. 'We can wait.' Then he would suck hard on his paintbrush or his pencil or whatever and say, 'I'll do some drawing.' I sometimes thought he drew because he was sexually frustrated. I wondered if I did give up my virginity, would he give up his art? But I was just looking for excuses. I knew we would be together, I just wasn't sure when. And I suppose I was nervous too. I didn't want to disappoint him.

On that day, I had been sitting with my friends on the sand and even though I wore a long skirt and cardigan – hardly beachwear – sand had found its way in and reached into places I didn't even know I had. And Callum? He asked to meet me later, saying, 'Let's knock about here for a while. My parents are home, so . . .'

There was nothing special about that day. I mean, nothing more special than my days with him usually were. Still, I remember it like it was yesterday.

Callum and I had walked out on the mud. The tide was out and the mud squelched around our ankles. I'll never forget the way it looked, like some primordial landscape. Streams of water ran through the clay and crabs and mud worms had surfaced to crawl about over the ripples of hard sand. Then we swam out on one of the river's tributaries. It didn't take long to get used to the cold water and we stayed in the sea for ages, chasing each other, splashing each other and pulling each other down. We nearly got trapped, but Callum held my hand and led me back to safety. A man in striped shorts hollered to us that the tide was coming in fast, and at that moment I decided – yes, it will be today that I give up my virginity. I don't know why it had to be that day and not the day before or after, but there was an indescribable tension in the air that contrasted with the innocence of the scene – mudlarking and splashing around.

It was as random as that.

So when we got back, our legs were covered in mud and sand and every kiss tasted of sea-salt. We lay down. Night had fallen and there was no one left on the beach. Callum still had to put away the last few deck-chairs but he said, 'Oh, let's forget about it,' and he drew me to him. He said he would sort it out later. I loved the way that he put me before his job. Especially that day.

I think Callum realised pretty quickly that I had decided. Maybe my kisses were more fervent or more impatient than usual. We skipped through the steps with much greater direction. We were 'goal-oriented', you might say. I remembered the man's warning: 'The tide is coming in fast . . .'

It was dark. If anyone was nearby they might have seen Callum parting my legs and looming over me, but I don't think there was anyone near enough. Callum's cock was hard, smooth and pointing right at me. I felt like he was a presenter and here was his mike: 'Now then, young lady, what do you think about this?' I had seen and touched his cock a million times before, but this was going to be different.

'I'll be as gentle as I can,' he whispered to me.

''S'all right,' I said, because I thought it would be. Not because I was a great horse rider or anything but I had been using tampons since I was twelve and, besides, there was all that rubbing on his bike. Surely that would make the difference?

I was wrong. It wasn't all right.

'Ahh, you're so tight,' Callum murmured as a real-live penis entered me for the first time. His breath was hot and wet in my ear.

'Is that good?' I said. I wasn't sure.

'Ye-es,' he breathed. 'Oh, yes.'

His cock slid right in, a series of bumpy shoves, like going over speed bumps, one, two, three, then it was right up me, and I thought I would explode.

'You're tighter than I thought,' he said, sounding pleased.

He filled me. I felt like he was in all the way up to my cheeks, in my head, I thought my eyes would pop out of their sockets. I mean, this felt tight beyond belief. And then he tried to move it. I could feel his cock deep inside me, like it was struggling, breathing in and out. Callum moved slowly, gently, forwards and back, forwards and back; and he hadn't reached the limit – he was going in deeper, ever deeper. How far inside me could he possibly get?

'Oh, fuck.' I wasn't sure what I was meant to feel but I was feeling something. It made me want to cry. I wanted to tell him to stop, please, but, at the same time, I was desperate for him not to stop. It made me wrap my legs around his back and make involuntary little noises. It made me want to dig my nails into his back. It made me want to hurt him. I could feel stones or shells jab into my bottom but I didn't care.

'Oh, yes!' I was flailing around on the sand. There might have been people wandering about, but I wanted him to know what I was feeling.

'Are you OK, baby?'

I couldn't answer. This was different from all the touching and playing we had done before. This was serious. This was a different league. He was swooping up and down on me like a bird, and I was helpless, yielding underneath. I locked my legs around his thighs and then I moved my legs higher. I clenched them around his back.

We were in our own world. We were on an island; it was just the two of us locked into our tiny world, wrapped up in each other, and he was pumping me so hard, it was more than I could stand. We had broken through the plateau and were running at the wall.

'Is this all right?' he asked.

I couldn't speak. I couldn't make sense of it. I was just able to groan my assent. I thought it was a groan, but it came out as more of a roar. 'Oh *yes*!' And then I was thrusting up against him, forcing him into a rhythm, forcing him in and out of me, so it wasn't him fucking me any more, it was me fucking him, or rather, both of us fucking each other.

Footsteps were scrunching on the sand nearby.

'Oh, Christ,' he said, 'someone's coming.'

But I hardly knew what he was saying for I was coming myself.

I spent the afternoon before the trek looking for things I would need, but since I didn't know what I needed it was quite pointless. I had boots and gloves and fleecy jackets. I had a hat and all that kind of thing. Anyway, I knew that I would be able to do the walk just fine. Some people feel at home with computers, some are at home in posh restaurants. With me it was mountains; I was just born that way. I couldn't help wondering how my Callum would cope.

4

The trek started at Pokhara, a small town in the foothills of the Himalayas. In Kathmandu the mules held up the road, bringing chaos to the traffic, but in this town it was the other way round. It was the half-built and neglected roads that held up the mules. The day we arrived there was a Tibetan demonstration and I watched as Callum spoke to the protesters. When he came back he was full of sympathy and I listened to him speaking eloquently about the situation but, I have to confess, all I was thinking about was how I could free *him* from his oppression and how *he* should be liberated. The world should not stand by and let Callum be treated in this way! When he asked me what I thought about it, I could hardly speak. I just said, 'Oh dear, what a problem!' He looked disappointed in me, so for the next couple of hours I worked hard at offering interesting opinions about everything to compensate for my lapse in intellect.

There were all sorts of people in Pokhara. Not just groups going on treks or returning from treks, although there were plenty of those, but there were hippies smoking roll-ups with sun-bleached kids in tow, and there were families up from India – families of up to five generations sometimes. The hippies and the Indian families ignored each other but in a way that spoke of familiarity.

Stella had said this was her favourite part of Nepal, and I could see why.

The day before we began the trek we took a boat out on the large lake that dominated the town; Chelle said this trip was to help us 'bond' before the big trip.

The water was flat and smooth. Even as we dipped the oars in and out, the surface barely rippled. There was an island in the middle of the lake and on it was a restaurant. Apparently it was very expensive and the former Nepalese royal family were frequent visitors. Chelle turned her nose up at the people who went there. 'How naff is that?' she exclaimed, but you could tell she really wanted to go.

Our guide, Raj, silently smoked his cigarettes. I had heard the Nepalese guides were good looking. He proved that theory wrong. His scowling face displayed evidence of years of acne and he had calves like boulders.

Callum stared at his sandals. I think he was still troubled by the Tibetan protesters. I loved the fact that he still cared about people; that he still was in touch with the world. I listened to Stella and Chelle, or rather I listened to Chelle talk about Chelle's job and Chelle's theory of the world and I pretended not to hear what they said but of course I did. I still had to work out what it was Chelle and Callum had in common.

Suddenly Chelle said, 'Every man needs a strong woman behind him. I'm a strong believer in that.'

'Oh?' said Stella.

'That's how it is with me and Cal. I am the power behind the scenes,' Chelle went on. 'I am his motor. He likes it that way.'

I decided that Callum probably had sex with Chelle in order to shut her up. 'Cal works hard. He's got his priorities right. He gives his all to his job. He'll be promoted within a year. I'll see to it that he is.'

I couldn't keep quiet any longer. 'Callum, don't you

paint?' The words 'any more' hung between us, a precarious ropeway.

Thrusting out her jaw, Chelle jumped in. 'No, why should he?'

'He looks like an artist,' I said meekly. 'That's all I meant.'

'There's no money in art.'

'Tell that to Damien Hirst,' I said.

'Well, we couldn't have this lifestyle if he were an artist. I love to travel. We wouldn't be able to if he wasn't in insurance.'

'This lifestyle'? 'Insurance'! Christ! The Callum I once knew, the beach boy, the motorbiker, the lover, would rather die than work in an office. I couldn't see him sat at a desk all summer with just a lap-top and a water-cooler for company. I couldn't see Callum thriving on team-building exercises. He used to say he would rather lose a limb than give up his art. Well, it looked like he had lost more than that; he had lost his mind. He used to say he saw everything as a picture. He used to want to create something everlasting, something everlasting that would make people think.

Well, he certainly had me thinking.

The water lapped at the side of the boat; this isn't a good idea. This isn't a good idea.

So much for bonding.

We started the trek without really realising that we had. One minute we were walking on a dusty road, the next we had turned on to a mountain path. It wasn't how you imagine trekking to be. I thought it was rather like walking in the English countryside. Stones and twigs crackled under us. Birds sang. I kept having to remind myself I was in Nepal and not in the Cotswolds.

'I can't believe I'm here,' I said to Stella. 'Thank you so much for persuading me.'

Stella clutched me awkwardly. She wasn't a huggy kind of girl, although you could tell she thought she ought to be.

'I'm so glad you came, Lauren. Aren't you glad?'

I supposed I was.

The further we went from the town, the more I relaxed. I concentrated on looking around and deep breathing. There was a lot to see and there was a lot of deep breathing to do. The air was different there. Everything was different. Except for Callum and Chelle that is. They walked side by side, even when the track was too narrow, and they didn't seem to want to talk with anyone else.

That evening we stopped at our first tea house. We had a dinner outside with a view over the entire valley. For the first time, I felt tremendously excited. Even if Callum were too occupied with Chelle – and perhaps that was too early to decide – I was still glad I had come. It was beautiful, with the mountains cradling us. It was just what I needed.

I didn't think I would sleep for my excitement but the bed was surprisingly comfortable and I drifted off pretty quickly. The next morning, Stella, who had shared a hut with me, said she didn't sleep at all and didn't I hear that noise all night? She said it was like a groaning sound, but it wasn't like someone was sick. I wondered if it was Callum and Chelle. They were on honeymoon, after all. The idea kind of spoiled my appetite for the curry and bread they served up for breakfast – not that I had much appetite anyway.

I was brushing my teeth in the shower rooms when Callum came up from behind. I saw him in the mirror but, when he saw me there, he hesitated and then turned back.

He was afraid of being alone with me.

By late afternoon the next day we were well and truly deep in the mountains and the scenery was somehow less like a Constable print and more like Middle Asia. It was growing cooler for a start. Raj and the two porters walked ahead with all our equipment while we straggled behind. Unlike Raj, the porters were, mercifully, quite attractive, so I anticipated some fun with them at least. The Nepalese seemed to almost glide on the paths while the rest of us had to march to keep up. Stella was slightly out of breath at the pace but she wouldn't slow down.

'This is normal,' she insisted. 'My body is adjusting.'

I noticed that Callum too was 'adjusting'. Sometimes he walked a stretch particularly quickly, just so that he could have a longer rest while waiting for us to catch up. Chelle though, like me, was barely affected by the change in speed. She strode out with her shoulders back, her tits forward – not that that achieved much.

'Having problems, Lauren?' she asked when I had slowed down to chat with Stella.

'Nothing I can't handle,' I snapped. I think it was only then I realised that this was a competition and Chelle was determined to win. But I supposed that was good in a way because maybe that meant that she hadn't won already.

The walk was more of a pleasure than I could have guessed. I loved the trails our feet made. I loved the way the houses at the foot of the mountain seemed to shrink smaller and smaller each time you looked at them and, like a child, you could only stare with your fingers curled in front of you and say, 'It's only this big.' I was almost happy.

Sometimes I went off alone, although it didn't seem to achieve anything but make me more aware than ever that there was no escaping myself. Wherever I went my longings and my dreams would come along with me. Geography changed nothing. There was all this magnificent scenery but no one with whom I could share it. (Stella didn't really count.) I didn't get to spend any time with Callum since Chelle never left him alone. She was never more than a handshake away from him. Did she even let him go to the toilet without her? The poor guy. He didn't stand a chance.

The leaves changed colour as we went higher. Occasionally there were signposts telling us how far we had come. Sometimes we passed little shrines to the gods, where someone had left a little sacrifice, flowers or foodstuffs. At first, I have to admit, I rushed past them – I didn't want Chelle to think I was slacking off – but then I thought, sod Chelle, and I slowed down. She wasn't going to spoil my enjoyment. Not too much anyway.

The vegetation became sparser. Things had to be pretty hardy to survive up there.

I watched Callum brush dead leaves out of Chelle's hair.

The porters told us stories and they never ran out of breath, or coughed up phlegm, or had to sit down, just for a minute, like we did. You would think we were barely moving from the way they chatted.

'I would like to marry an English girl,' one of them said. He looked away from me and blushed. It wasn't the first time I had made him blush. Not that I was interested, of course. I was a one-guy gal even if my guy was a one-gal guy. Still, the boy was quite handsome, although I think he was frighteningly young, not much more than eighteen or nineteen.

'Really?' said Chelle, as if nothing ever surprised her. 'So that you can go and live in England?'

'No, so I could share my beautiful country with her.'

Chelle didn't say anything.

It *was* beautiful though. You could see why they wouldn't want to leave.

They talked about their families and their schools and the things they wanted to do this year and next. I thought they must have told these stories to the millions of trekkers hiking through their country, but they weren't disillusioned or resentful of us. They simply accepted us.

I looked at Callum stroking Chelle's wrists. Maybe it was about time I started accepting a few things.

We met a group who were on their way down. They told us they had been up the north slopes.

'The view was fantastic. It was the best ever. Better than this even,' they said. Later, we met another group who said they were on the way back from Everest base camp. It had taken about twelve days to get there from where we were.

'It was amazing,' one said, and the rest of them nodded their heads vigorously. 'You couldn't leave Nepal without visiting base camp, could you?'

This made Chelle get even more self-important than usual. Raj went into a huddle with the two porters and then they all came back to us shaking their heads very seriously. They said we weren't prepared. Our clothes were too light. We weren't 'professionals'.

That word was like a red rag to one old bull . . .

'But it's fine,' she insisted. 'We are all fit, aren't we? We can handle it. What has a professional got that we haven't?'

But the porters weren't sure. Nor was Callum. He took Chelle aside and although I don't think we were meant to hear, he said something like, 'Everest isn't a hobby, babe. It isn't something you can do without preparation.'

'I know that!' Chelle retorted loudly. She talked to Callum like he was a little boy. 'But we're not talking about going *up* Everest, it's just base camp.'

'But what's the point?'

'It's about being part of the atmosphere, of course!'

Poor Callum. He didn't belong in this climate. The situation wasn't him. I'm not saying he wasn't a daredevil, he was, but not in a physical way. Didn't Chelle know that? Didn't Chelle know him at all?

'It's still a bloody long way up,' Callum tried weakly.

'God, Callum, don't you get anything?'

I know it's not funny when a couple who are the embodiment or advertisement of domestic bliss and harmony have a ruck in public, but it gave me a secret thrill. Or maybe not so secret.

'What *are* you grinning about?' Stella poked me in the small of my back.

'Nothing...'

'Don't be nasty, Lauren.'

'I'm not. I'm just being part of the atmosphere. God, Stella –' I made my voice like Chelle's '– don't you get anything?'

We walked ten kilometres a day. We had found a compromise, although I don't know who was involved in the decision-making. Compromise seemed to be just another way our resident bully used to enforce the rules. The plan was that we would walk towards base camp but we could 'turn around at any point.' I'm sure we couldn't though. Chelle ruled us like unruly schoolkids and you really wouldn't want to be the one to let down her team.

The youngest porter chatted to me and offered to take my hand when the going got rough.

'Does it get very rough?' I asked. I couldn't resist flirting with him just a little. He was so young and so very sincere. Anyway, I had to flirt with him because the others had zero appeal. (I had gone off the other porter when I saw him laughing as he beat a chicken over its head.) This man won hands-down.

'Yes, ma'am,' he said.

'Do you like it rough?'

He blushed. 'Now you are teasing me!'

'No,' I said, because I suddenly felt guilty because I wasn't interested in him and although it did cross my mind that maybe I could try to make Callum jealous, I knew Callum well enough to know that Callum did not do jealousy.

Sometimes, as Chelle marched ahead, she tried to 'keep up our spirits' with songs and words of wisdom from one of her books. I had seen her reading her books before. They all had titles like *Professional Women Can Find Harmony*, or *How to be Successful and Calm*, or *Why Happiness is Refusing to be a Doormat*.

'Lauren,' Chelle called out, 'have you ever thought that you might want to smile now and again?'

I'm afraid I did do jealousy. I was a PhD in the subject. Sometimes I wanted to slap Chelle around her successful and calm face. That way I was sure this doormat could find harmony.

Callum would shrug at me and it might have been my imagination but I'm sure, once or twice, he raised his eyes heavenward as if he was saying 'What can I do with her?'

As I walked, I dreamed how it would be if only Chelle

was out of the picture. I had two favourite scenarios that I kept returning to. They both revolved around massage. This wasn't as daft as it sounded because with all the walking that was what you tended to think about. Potentially, I told myself, this *could* come true.

Scenario 1: I walk into Callum's hut. I am wearing my tight jeans and an even tighter T-shirt. 'My legs hurt,' I say. He tells me he will massage my legs but I must take off my jeans. I am not happy to do this but, oh, very reluctantly, I take down my trousers. He massages my calves. I tell him it feels good. He asks if he should go higher. I tell him he might do, if it's no bother. He tells me it is no bother. He asks me to lie down and he presses on my thighs. His fingers are exploring a little higher. I turn around. We embrace. I take off my T-shirt, impress him with my whoppers.

He pushes his face into my chest. We fuck.

Scenario 2: Callum walks into my hut. He comes out with the same opening line. 'My legs hurt.' I am wearing – hmm – no, I have just had a shower and only have on my underwear. For modesty's sake, however, I am wrapped in a towel. I say that my legs hurt too, but he ignores me, gets on my bed and I start touching him. He is lying on his stomach, his face buried in the pillow. He tells me it smells good. I ask him what it smells of and he says it smells of me. I massage his thighs. I let my fingers drift in between. I can see his balls through his pants. His balls are bigger than I remember.

'I missed you,' he says.

'Oh?' I am cool. I carry on the massage, yet I am stretched over his body, I am sitting over his arse. OK, I should be massaging his legs but I am massaging his back for some reason. My hands are moving down. I have to touch his balls.

Callum turns over, only this is magic, and just as

how a magician can pull a tablecloth yet the plates all stay in the same place, so I too am in the same place, only now, of course, I am straddling his crotch. 'Christ, I've missed you.' I'm not sure if he should say, 'I've missed you' or if he will say, 'I've missed these' to my tits. I'm not sure if this is passionate or romantic. I think today we will go for the passionate. I undo my bra. This is the twenty-first century after all. His fingers are inside me. I tell him, 'Callum, fuck me hard.'

And he does.

Stella pushed me lightly.

'A penny for your thoughts, Lauren.'

'Thanks for interrupting them. Things were just getting interesting.'

'In that case,' she smirked, 'it's good I stopped you. We can't have you getting too carried away. I think that young man has a soft spot for you.'

'What young man?' I said quickly, for I thought she meant Callum. I realised my mistake as soon as I had said it.

'I mean the porter, you idiot.' Stella didn't look impressed.

'Oh, right,' I said flatly. 'Great!'

'I've heard rumours,' she said. It was quite unlike her. She didn't usually like talking about men or stuff like that. I think her sex-drive was in neutral. Or perhaps even reverse. 'The porters pride themselves on giving girls more than just a lift up to the top.'

I couldn't stop laughing. 'Come on. He's just a baby! What could he do?'

Before Stella could reply, Chelle had started off on another round of ten green bottles and we all had to join in with the 'hanging on a wall'.

* * *

In the evening at the tea house we warmed our hands around little candles on the outdoor tables. I loved the tea houses. Arriving at a tea house was my favourite moment of the day. At this one, the mother cooked while the children served us the food and drinks and asked us to show where we were from on a big map pinned over the table. The father would be home soon. He was a guide – 'somewhere up there,' the mother said, pointing to the highest mountain in the Anapurna circuit. The mother's skin was prematurely aged but she never stopped smiling. We got to meet other people there too: groups of trekkers coming down, groups coming across. No one else was going up though; apparently it was too late in the season. Chelle told them all that we were going to base camp and they looked impressed. One of the guys looked sceptical though.

'I thought you had to be professionals to do that,' he said.

Raj shrugged. 'Maybe.'

Chelle lapped it up.

The young porter chatted to the girls in the other group. They seemed to like him. He put his arm on their shoulders and they leaned into him. I couldn't stop watching him now. What did the porters give the girls? I wondered. Or, rather, what could a skinny lad like him possibly give me? He had surprisingly light eyes, almost translucent or grey and his teeth weren't as bad as some of the other locals I'd seen. Sometimes, when he was listening hard, he stuck his tongue between his teeth and I could see it, all little, pink and soft. It reminded me of the inside of a shell.

'I wouldn't be surprised if our children turn out to be Olympic athletes or something,' Chelle said to me as we cleaned our hands side by side at the cold tap before our dinner of goat curry. 'That kind of thing is genetic.'

'Oh?' I said. I kept my fingers under the water. It was freezing but I didn't want to take my hands out just yet. Their children? Callum and she were going to have children?

'Callum's family is quite sporty too.'

I used to love Callum's family. They were so different from mine. They didn't just lumber in front of the TV but did things: sailing, cycling and horse-riding. They had parties and barbecues. They kissed each other hello, goodbye, mwah, mwah.

'I know,' I said.

'How do *you* know?' She was quick, I'll say that for her. Callum was chatting with the porters on the other side of the house. They were teaching him how to make a fire or something. I could have told Chelle everything. I could have sparked up our own fire here. Of course I didn't though.

'I mean, I can imagine,' I said. 'He's quite ... hearty, isn't he?'

'Hearty?' She laughed. She rubbed her hands brusquely. They were bright red.

'He's not a bloody fried breakfast. He's much more than hearty, I can tell you. Callum is hung like a donkey. Why do you think I married him?'

To ride on Callum's motorbike, I rolled up my navy school skirt at the waist so that it lightly skimmed my thighs. I liked the feeling, or rather the non-feeling, of an ultra-short skirt. I didn't worry about my top half. I kept on the school uniform of pale blue shirt, the navy and yellow stripy tie. I also had to wear the school's thick navy knickers and each one had my name sewn into the elastic along the top.

I walked out through the school gates and, with everyone's eyes on me, I made my way to Callum proudly. I kissed him not only so that everyone knew we were together but also because he was my boyfriend, my beautiful Callum, and he deserved every kiss he got. He would kiss me back, sometimes for ages, sometimes for just a second, and then he would pass me my helmet.

'Come on, get on.'

Callum was at art college by then and he was loving it. I worried at the girls, all those bohemian model-types, but he said, 'No way, José.' He didn't think my age was a disadvantage. 'You're not immature,' he said. 'Christ, it's only two years! Why do you make such a big deal?'

But I did always feel that my school uniform told the world just how mature I really was.

One day, while kissing me, he felt his way around my school skirt, yes, there in the street, and then he groaned. 'You're not wearing those big navy knickers again.'

'What of it? I have to wear them for school.'

'Take them off. You're not in the classroom now.'

How dared he talk to me like that? The newborn feminist inside me raged. I had just been reading *The Second Sex* and *A Woman's Room* and I was up in my sixteen-year-old arms. Like I would do anything he said, just because he said it! Who did he think he was?

'You want me to take them off?' I said, just checking to see if he really was that cheeky.

'Yeah, get 'em off. Right now.'

It was delicious. I walked over to a bush and peeled the knickers down my legs and stuffed them into my rucksack. I came back to him beaming.

'Done. Do you want to see?'

'I believe you.' He revved the motor. Before he pulled down the visor, he winked.

I got on the bike and instantly felt different. I could

feel the opening of my pussy and everything was vibrating beneath it. It was never unpleasant being on the back of the bike with the engine vibrating against me but this was a new category of enjoyment. I leaned right over so that my clit was rubbing against the seat.

'What are you doing?'

'Nothing!'

'You're rubbing yourself, aren't you?'

'Maybe.'

'Sit up straight, baby. It's dangerous.'

'I can't,' I said. I really couldn't. It felt so good.

At the red lights, Callum turned around. The engine was making the seat pulse.

'Are you still doing that, Lauren?'

'No . . . I . . .'

'You're crazy, you know that?'

'I'm crazy about you,' I said. My cheeks were burning but he wouldn't have known that because the helmet obscured most of my face.

That time, he didn't take me back to his house but took me to the cliffs of the marine parade, where we fucked up against a tree. He had to get into quite an odd position so that his cock could get inside me. I was gripping the trunk so hard that bits of bark came off in my hands. He sucked the tongue out of me and I bit the side of his neck. I wanted to show him how much I was affected.

Then he turned me over. He made me support myself on my hands and knees and fucked me from behind. I didn't know what to make of it. I had dandelions in my face and mouth and he was standing behind me, one hand resting on the small of my back, and I could hear him breathing and sighing his pleasure. Then he put one hand on my breast and pulled at the nipple and something really animal came over me. And Chelle was right. He was hung like a donkey. Only back then I didn't know it. I didn't have the means of comparison. I didn't know just how precious that was; all I knew was that he felt tight and deep and perfect. I started to push back into him, as hard and fast as I could, harder and faster, and I wasn't even aware what was going on, where he was, where we were or anything.

Chelle didn't love Callum; never had. What a thing to say about my man! I mean, it wasn't *nasty* as such, it was a compliment in a way, but Callum was much more than just a big dick, that was for sure. But when I told Stella what Chelle had said, she said that *I* was the one who was being immature. Chelle was only joking, Stella insisted. 'Why are you so down on her?' she asked, but I didn't reply.

Although the food at that tea house was the best we had had so far, and although the views were awesome, they didn't have many real facilities there. They didn't even have a shower. We couldn't wash properly. And from now on, it was just the water we were carrying. Raj kept warning us that conditions would get more primitive the higher up we went.

More primitive? I repeated the idea to myself. I didn't think that would be such a bad thing. I suppose my expression gave my thoughts away because the young porter winked at me.

'Don't worry, I'll look after you,' he said.

I couldn't believe how arrogant he was. Really, he was just a boy!

Apparently, after a few more days, there would be no more tea houses as the people who run them would all head south for the winter. We would, Raj explained, have to camp.

Callum asked quietly, 'Shouldn't we head south too?

Doesn't that mean the climbing season has ended?' But Chelle clapped her hands.

'I love tents. And I love making love in a tent. It's so snug and cozy, like going back to the womb.'

Was it only me who noticed that Callum's skin had turned quite green?

That night, the air was thick with the wail of mountain wolves, but I thought I heard Callum and Chelle having sex. I pictured them in the adjacent hut, him on top of her. I thought about his buttocks going up and down, pumping in and out. Her nipples would be hard as a rock face between his fingers. He would pump her full, like the animals we saw on the way up. I tried to block the thought out – we had a heavy day of walking ahead – but I grew hot and wet. I tried to imagine that it was Raj with his acne-beaten face and sullen glances, or perhaps it was the young porter, with his long eyelashes and his soft tongue who was making love to me, but my fantasies just boomeranged back to him, bloody Callum.

5

The trek grew arduous. Sometimes the porters had to cut through the branches to make a path, and sometimes we had to use our hands to pull ourselves up. It became colder too. It wasn't too uncomfortable but we definitely needed to wear a couple of jumpers and Stella and I put on thick tights under our jeans. I was still more than happy to be up in the mountains though. I especially liked the morning light. Watching the sun's slow rise over the valleys was tremendous and made me think that I would never see the world in the same way again. There was no way I could fit in my old routine after experiencing this.

One morning, the young porter bounded over to me and told me which mountain was which. I told him to go and tell Stella. I think she then sent him over to Callum and Chelle. I explained that I preferred to be on my own, but that was only half-true. I preferred to be on my own than with him, but my number one preference would have been to be with Callum, of course.

As I walked I reworked my two scenarios with the enthusiasm of a first-time film director. I changed the lighting; sometimes the events took place in the morning, not the evening. I changed the outfits; in one of them I found myself in stockings and suspenders, here in Nepal! I added and then took away props – Stella's handy pen-light, a candle or two. The only things I didn't change were the actors. It was always Callum and me, and the same conclusion. The story always ended with us having sex. Sometimes I would catch myself thinking not only about Callum and the leg massaging scenarios but also about the temple. I couldn't stop thinking about the image of the woman being tied up and fucked by all those men in robes. Who was it? Did she survive it? What would it feel like?

I came across Stella a few yards up. She said she was taking photos of the view but she didn't have her camera. She looked a bit flustered. She said she didn't know I was behind her; she thought I had gone ahead.

'What's up?' I asked.

'Nothing special,' she said, but she wouldn't meet my eyes.

I assumed it was something to do with Callum and Chelle, but when I asked, Stella looked annoyed and threw herself on to the grass to the side of the path.

'The world doesn't revolve around them, you know,' she said. I tried to think of something the world did revolve around.

'Stella, do you ever think about what we saw? At the temple that time?'

'What do you mean?'

I told Stella how I couldn't get the woman out of my mind. The way she was lying there with her legs spread. And in the first panel, she was with one man but in the second and in the third there were lots of them and she was taking it everywhere . . . 'and I mean everywhere,' I said, my voice trailing away as I saw Stella had her uptight look on again.

'Sounds painful,' Stella said, and I could tell she was embarrassed. Stella was the wrong person to talk to about this kind of thing; she really hated sex-talk. I couldn't stop myself though. Callum used to say I was like a dog with a bone when I got going. He used to like that about me.

'Yes, but don't you remember her face? It was like she was in Nirvana or something.'

Stella went red and said she hadn't noticed a thing.

Then Chelle came over at us, out of nowhere. She said, 'Did you lose your way?' and neither Stella nor I said another word about the temple.

That evening, the mountains were even more magnificent than they had ever appeared before; they didn't disappear in the shadow of night but were darker than the sky – huge hulking shapes that would never go away. And the stars were magical. I sat on the grass outside the huts, wishing I could just sink into them and lose myself in the view. And then another hut door opened and a figure emerged. I don't know how I managed to hold down my smile as I saw it was Callum and that he was tiptoeing in the dark towards me.

'Hey!'

'I couldn't sleep,' he said. It sounded like he was making an excuse. Why did he have to give excuses? Didn't he remember fucking me against the trees, the bark in my hair? Couldn't he remember the way I pushed against him or the way I used to gasp his name?

'Nor could I,' I said, hugging myself.

'It's hard to sleep up here,' he said.

We both couldn't sleep. I hoped it was for the same reason: we were both thinking about each other. If only I could get rid of the old bat he was attached to, we'd be romping home.

'Isn't this something?' He sat next to me, again leaving a 'safe' distance between us, and then he contemplated the sky. I remembered that it was Callum who taught me about the stars. That night on the beach after we made love for the first time, he told me about the Great Bear, the Southern Cross, the Pleiades and Orion.

I reminded him, but his answer was a bit of a disappointment.

'I was making it up.' He shrugged. 'I didn't really know which one was which. I had just heard the names.'

I don't know if it was his intention to try to hurt me, but it did. What a shit-head, I thought. Chelle could keep him.

It was burning cold but I didn't want to go inside yet. I kept telling Callum that, and I wondered how he would interpret it: would he think it was a simple 'I don't want to go in yet' – or would he look for the deeper meaning? And there was a deeper meaning, of course. Couldn't he just hold my hand? Maybe lightly brush my breasts or something? I could live with that. I could live with the idea of us seducing each other all over again. I wanted to be adored – the way Chelle was, I suppose, even though she mostly adored herself.

'What are you thinking?' he asked.

'The stars are so beautiful,' I lied. 'Whatever they're called. I don't care. They don't need a label, do they?'

He nodded. I don't think he was really listening to me.

'What are you thinking about, then?' I added. (The what-are-you-thinking question is one of those questions you really have to answer.)

'Just how nice this is.'

'Nice?' I said. 'I was told never to use the word nice.'

'Who told you that?'

'You, probably. You were the one who taught me most things.'

He smiled. I don't know if he was deliberately ignoring the innuendo or not. 'I think you know what I mean. Anyway, are you too cold?'

'No, I'm absolutely fine.'

I seemed to have acquired some kind of compulsive hide-the-truth disorder. Of course I was cold. I was fucking freezing. Instead of thermals I was wearing my best underwear. This was a red see-through ensemble. My pubes looked like black plants pressed up against a window. I imagined them calling, 'Let us out, let us out.' I didn't think it was a look that would catch on in Nepal.

Christ, I needed a shag. Today, the porters had talked about reincarnation. Chelle was sure she was a great female warrior in a past life. I must have been a prostitute who died of some nasty disease. Or maybe I was New Gwynn. Come to think of it, that sounded fun!

'I take it you're feeling a bit on the nippy side?' I said.

'Yeah. And you must be too, Lauren. You're not made of ice, are you?'

This time, my teeth chattered an answer for me.

'Well, come here, then.' He held out his arm and I snuggled in place. *My* place.

And, Christ, I wasn't going to feel guilty about Chelle. No way. Not after the look she gave me this afternoon when I was talking with Stella.

'That's OK, isn't it?'

I nodded my head in his arm. He must have felt my answer. Mmm. This was almost as good as my leg-massaging story. It was different but the conclusion might be the same. Besides, he still might claim that his legs ached. Or I could.

'I won't bite,' he added. Shit, I thought – he won't bite.

He felt so good and he smelled good too. I put my head on his chest and felt his arms wrap around me, clutch me to him. I felt warm and, for the first time in a long time, I felt safe.

But his mouth, his gorgeous heart-shaped mouth,

was only five or six inches away, but it might as well have been in a different country for all that I could reach it. I didn't dare myself to raise my head. What if he didn't want to kiss me? His wife was sleeping in the tent next door.

'My legs ache,' I said.

'Yeah, well we've walked a long way,' he said casually.

Damn, he wasn't supposed to say that. But still he hadn't left my side.

'Are you enjoying yourself?' His leather jacket was soft against my jumper.

'What, this? You mean this?'

He laughed. 'No, I meant the trip. Are you having a good time?' His right hand made patterns on my back. Did the patterns symbolise something? What were they saying? I was freezing but I wouldn't have missed this for the world. This was *better* than the scenarios I had imagined. Sod the fantasy, I had to get real. He might have his own ideas about how he wanted things to proceed.

'It's good.'

'Good? Is that all?'

What kind of underwear would he be wearing? It took my breath away to think about it. I pushed myself closer to him. Couldn't he feel my breasts pressed against him? Didn't it affect him at all?

'It's great.'

'You say that like there's a problem.'

'There is.'

He didn't stop massaging my back for a moment. I looked at my thighs and I think he did too. I wanted him to put his hand on my knee.

'This is quite weird for me,' he said eventually.

'What is?'

'Oh, nothing.'

Callum took his hand away from my back and shivered.

'This cold and me ... don't seem to get on. Not like you. You really do look at home here.'

'Thank you, I think,' I said. Then he came out with something that stopped me short.

'I can't stop looking at you sometimes. I'm sorry.'

'That's OK,' I said calmly. (OK? It was fucking marvellous!)

'It's no big deal,' he added.

'Oh?'

'It's just Chelle. I wouldn't want to upset her. I don't want her to get jealous.'

'She's got no reason to be jealous,' I said. 'Has she?'

'Not really, no.'

Now that was settled, Callum tightened his fingers around me, and this time I snuggled deeper into the corners of him, the creases of him. I kept my eye on his crotch all the time. Would I be able to tell if he got a boner? Maybe he had one now? No, we were only chatting, for God's sake.

He laughed, suddenly, abruptly, like a shooting star.

'What are you laughing at?' I asked.

'This!'

'What?'

'Us, here.'

'Pretty funny.'

This was the moment; this was the moment we might begin again. But Callum buried his face in his hands.

'I really wish you got on well with Chelle.'

Why did he want us to be friends? I thought. Men always did, and that really was too much to ask.

'She's very ... nice. I like her,' I managed to struggle out.

Callum gave this little sound that suggested I didn't know the half of it. 'She really is. She thinks you're depressed, Lauren. She thinks you need looking after. That's why I'm out here.'

'That's very ... very kind of her.'

'Well, that's Chelle all over. You know, she's always so considerate. You know she's really impressed with Stella. She's thinking about doing charity work too now.'

'Right,' I said. *As if!* That cow work for a charity? Pigs *don't* fly.

'I'm sorry I didn't tell her about you. I just don't want her to know. I just don't. If you felt anything for me then you'd accept that.'

'OK, OK.'

'Well, that's that then.'

'Don't go,' I said. 'Not yet.' Not back to her. Not back to her when you could have me.

'Look, this is getting a bit ...'

'What?'

'Heavy.'

'It doesn't have to be. Let's talk about something else then.'

'What else is there?' he said, and I knew, at least I thought I knew, he felt the same. I met his mouth with mine, and I kissed him. I was hesitant at first but I kissed him again and then again and again until I felt he was kissing me. He tilted my head back and kissed me and initially they were soft kisses, like snowdrops on to my lips, again and again, and then they grew harder, more passionate, and our mouths fell open and his tongue poked into my mouth and mine into his. He was swirling around the wetness of my mouth, and I was doing it back to him, and I was wet down there between my legs, like I hadn't been for ages and I felt so unworried, so relaxed. It felt so natural, but in a fantastic way, like everything was hyper-real.

'Don't you think it's killing me, being here with you but not being here *with* you?' he whispered into my mouth.

He kissed me again really hard, and he grabbed my hand and put it on his cock. I swear to God he hadn't changed, and it hadn't been my imagination playing tricks. He really was as fantastically large as he ever was, only this time around I knew I was going to really appreciate it. His tongue was hot and slippery, probing my mouth, and it almost made me cry out. I massaged his cock, feeling that erection, loving that erection. He put his hand on my thigh.

I let out an encouraging groan. Don't stop now, Callum, I thought. If I was a prostitute in a past life, I bet I was a bloody good one. Maybe I made a fortune and opened my own brothel. Maybe Callum was my favourite customer. Maybe Chelle was one of my minions and I shouted at her, tellng her she wasn't appealing enough to the clientele.

'Darling,' he said.

'We should be together,' I breathed into his mouth. That was all I could say. His fingers had reached the top of my thigh and all I could think was please, please, touch me there.

Then suddenly his fingers were gone. It felt like they had been ripped away from me.

'Callum?' It was Chelle. My heart plummeted. 'What are you doing?'

'I'm just talking to Lauren, sweet. I won't be a minute.'

'OK, baby. I'll keep the bed deliciously warm. Just the way you like it.'

She turned away.

What an absolute pain in the arse she was.

6

I was raging when I went back to the hut. Something had been about to happen with Callum but that bloody Chelle had got in the way. She had scuppered my plans and I hated her for that. How could Callum want to spend his time with her? Was she really so hot in bed? I found it hard to believe.

'What on earth is the matter?' Stella asked. I stormed in sulkily. She was brushing her hair. The electricity made it fly.

'This is just so ... so weird.' Weird was the only way I could describe it. Out there it felt so right with Callum and yet Chelle's appearance showed us that it wasn't that simple.

'It's this place, Lauren. It sends people a little crazy. They say the mountains can haunt you. There are just so many and you can never get to the top of them all. So high up and yet ... Actually, I had a dream you were surrounded by demons and you couldn't get away.'

She had a dream about me? Sometimes Stella could say some weird things too. Maybe she was the one who was a little crazy. I wondered what she would have been in a past life, assuming, of course, that there was such a thing. I wondered if you could change sex between lives. I read somewhere that most men would choose to come back as a woman. Probably so they could spend the whole day playing with their breasts!

Stella was gazing at me, concerned I was going to

tell her my thoughts on reincarnation, but I changed my mind.

Maybe she was a eunuch in a past life. I'm sure she didn't have sex.

'I'll be OK. Any demons that are chasing me are in here.' I patted my heart.

'So what is it?'

'I just can't stop thinking about Callum.'

She nodded at me to continue. Her eyebrows were furrowed. She looked really sad.

'I tried to forget him,' I admitted. 'I really did. It seems to be getting worse, not better. All I want to do is reach out and grab him.'

'Everyone feels like this about their first love,' Stella said. 'I'm sure everyone wants to go back and shag them again. It's quite normal.'

The word 'shag' sounded funny coming from her.

'Not everyone.' I didn't know when I had started shouting. 'Name one other person who feels this way.' Just in case she could, I added, 'Or two or three other people, go on, who feel like this.'

Since Stella and I didn't have any mutual friends, I might as well have said, 'What do you know? It's not like you ever have sex,' for that was what I really was thinking.

But Stella knew how to treat me. 'Tell me,' she said softly. She put down her hairbrush. The bristles were caught with hair. 'What made Callum so special?'

Callum, Callum, Callum. He wasn't like the other boys I knew. Girls at school said that relationships changed if you 'let the boys have sex with you'. The story went that 'boys lose respect' but I thought it deepened everything. Our sex was the best thing in the world. Each time we fucked was pure wonderment. We had found something so amazing. We had discovered treasure, or the next wonder of the world. We played and we experimented. He tied me up and licked me. I hand-cuffed him and sucked him. He fingered me on the bus. He said we should call that 'a 43', in honour of the bus route. The two old ladies in front had no idea why I was squirming in the seat. He called me his dirty girl and it made the shivers down my spine even worse. I gave him a blow-job in a taxi. I knew the driver was watching us with a dirty grin but I didn't care and Callum, well, he cared, but there was nothing he could do about it.

It wasn't just sex. Of course it wasn't.

We talked about everything and everyone. I had never talked so much in my life. The only time we stopped talking was when we were fucking and even then we didn't stop, we were so full of 'fuck-me's', and 'harder' and 'mores' our tongues never got a real rest.

He was sweet to me. He gave me presents, and I don't just mean the odd Quality Street or daffodils from a petrol station. Callum's presents were lavish. It started the first Christmas we were together and never really stopped. That Christmas, the presents just kept coming and so did we. We kept running off to be alone together; he gave me 43s in the kitchen next to the turkey. I gave him a blow-job in the bathroom while his great uncle knocked on the door outside.

Each time he bought me a new item of clothing, I would put it on and twirl around for him. I was hungry for his gifts – not so much for the presents themselves as for what I knew they meant. These were carefully thought-out presents and each one represented how much Callum loved and respected me. I didn't know how he could afford them – he wasn't selling much of his art – but he told me not to worry, 'It is taken care of.' I didn't worry anyway. It was perfect to be wearing such exquisite things under my school uniform. Can you imagine white satin French knickers and a French camisole under a frumpy school skirt and blouse? Callum liked me in white best; he said I was his snow queen, his ice princess, only the best for his girl. I still have a necklace he got for me from that time, although I threw most of the other stuff away.

After he gave me my present for the week (later, they became more frequent and it became 'a present for being so lovely', or 'a present for being his girlfriend'), he kissed my hair and said it smelled nice. He brushed it away from my forehead just so that he could see me better. He knew how to touch me down there too. He knew that I liked to keep my knickers on, not up, but still on, so that they stretched around my knees, so that I couldn't open my legs really wide, only wide enough, and always wide enough. And I liked him to look; I liked to show him everything. I may have been young but I understood that a man likes to see where he is going.

Sixteen years I had been without him. Sixteen years, and yes, I had managed. I had gone weeks and months without thinking of him. But each time a relationship ended, Callum came back to haunt me. His kisses, his cock, his presents, all came back. Then, seconds after the happy memories returned, back came Rose Connelly and the way she and he had made me feel.

'He was just different, that's all.' I looked at Stella, but she was looking down. She picked at her nails, not that they were dirty or anything. Stella was always washing her hands. She had nice healthy nails. I liked the clearness of her moons.

'You obviously loved Callum an awful lot but you

have to consider, maybe he's not the only one for you now and . . .'

'And what?'

'Callum is not the kind of guy to play around.'

Who said anything about playing?

'How do you know?'

'Things Chelle has said.'

'So you've talked to her about it?'

'Course not. Look, let's forget about this and go to sleep.'

'Who else is there for me, anyway?'

She gave me a look. She didn't mean the young porter, did she? He was so short he didn't count. He barely came up to my tits!

'If you don't know that, then I'm not going to tell you,' she said.

She *did* mean the young porter. Pathetic!

'Well . . . I'm going to get Callum. If Chelle hadn't come along just then we would have been fucking right now.'

'I'm sure you're right,' Stella said, but I could tell she didn't think it was a great thing.

The next day, even though Callum and I stayed away from each other, it felt to me like we were closer than ever. We had kissed, and we would have gone on kissing all night if Chelle hadn't showed up. We would have gone on to goodness knows what. And that meant something, I knew it did. All the same, it *was* weird to be with him. He so didn't fit in the mountain environment. He was like a black and white character caught in a colour film. That morning I walked along in a Technicolor state of high arousal. The slightest brush against my skin, like when some branches tapped my back, made me shiver. Still it seemed to make me walk up that mountain even quicker. Like if you add oil to a difficult door and you find it opens much more easily, now that I knew Callum was looking at me sometimes it made things so different! And thinking about what he'd said made me feel all warm and excited.

Of course, in a past life Callum would have been magnificent. Maybe he had something to do with the sea. Yes, that was it; he was an adventurer, exploring tropical islands, returning with potatoes or pineapples or somesuch. And I was Queen Elizabeth the First. He would lay down his coat for us to make love on in front of all my admiring courtiers. Well a girl has got to dream, hasn't she?

It was getting much colder. Now we wore coats, gloves and hats. Stella had lost her hat and there was a big hoo-hah about it but, in the end, the young porter sorted something out. I quite liked him for that.

'I sort you out later, too,' he said, nudging my arm.

'Oooh,' I said, looking at Callum and wondering if he had noticed. 'But I already have a hat,' I told him.

'I don't mean that,' he said, although I didn't need his explanation. 'I mean, I can keep you warm, if you like.'

'I'm fine,' I said. 'Thanks for the offer though.'

I think Callum was too busy playing 'I-spy' at that moment to see that other people were interested in me; to see that actually it wasn't only me who had a rival. He had one too. But when no one had guessed Chelle's phrase was 'hiking boots' (full marks to Chelle!) it was Callum's turn. He thought for a moment and only then did he turn to acknowledge me. He was staring at my tits. But he could hardly say, 'Something beginning with L's Ts', now could he?

'It's your turn,' Chelle reminded him. 'God, Callum, keep up.'

I didn't get a moment alone with him. I almost did when Stella went to look at some wild purple flowers and Chelle went galloping off with her, but by the time I had slithered down the stony path to be next to him, Chelle was by his side again. Her fingers were in his fingers and her smug smile was all over her face. I decided that, even if there were no past lives, there was definitely a future life. Chelle would be an ant and, oops! I seem to have trodden on her.

Fortunately we were to enjoy timber rather than canvas shelter that night. Raj said there was a storm coming. We all wondered how he knew. There had been no change in the sky. The clouds floated above us harmoniously like swans on water. The silence was no more threatening than usual. Even the birds weren't flying off and leaving us. They were doing exactly what they always did. Did Raj have some supernatural powers to know such things?

'I heard it on the radio,' he eventually explained, showing us his tiny transistor.

'A storm! Excellent!' Chelle said, when we had stopped laughing. 'That'll be something to tell the folks at home, won't it?'

Callum's face was a lighter shade of pale. 'Are you sure we should be going up?'

Raj shrugged. 'You pay, I do.'

I didn't expect Chelle to respond the way she did. 'Stop bothering them, Cal,' she said. 'Where's your sense of adventure?'

It made me think that perhaps the storm was the last of their worries.

At nine o'clock that evening, straight after another curry dinner, I announced that I was going to bed. 'I probably won't be able to sleep though,' I said. Everyone looked up surprised. I had been hoping to convey to Callum that I would see him tonight, maybe at eleven again, but I realised I would have to be more obvious. I went over to kiss him goodnight. I put my lips to his cheek. He was shaving much less than usual and his face had a spiky feel. I didn't want to pull away.

'Callum,' I whispered.

'We need to ... talk,' he said.

'I've never heard it called that before,' I whispered back. He smiled at me limply.

'I ...'

'I'm joking. Can we meet later?'

'What is it, Lauren?' interrupted Chelle. I don't know how she moved across the room so fast. Her hair was flat from where her hat had been.

I said, 'I'm just ... challenging Callum to a game of I-spy'

'Can't we all play?' she asked.

I groaned inside.

'Yes,' Callum called after me softly. 'Tonight. I'll be there.'

I lay on my sleeping bag. I could hear Stella and the others still at the dinner table and I could hear their laughter. It wasn't until just before midnight that the place fell quiet. I counted to one hundred – just for luck – and then left the hut. I hoped that Callum and I would get a chance for a sneaky shag. It was important to me that we got the first time right so that he would know it was worth the inevitable upheaval and chaos that would ensue if Chelle found out. Would we rush in passionately or would we do it slow and romantic? What did he want? I didn't want him to ask me. I wanted him to know without asking, and yet I myself didn't know. I decided that under the circumstances –

we were two miles up and freezing cold – fast was the answer. Rapid application of mouth on throat, followed by hands up tops, cock out and inserted and *voila*! Beneath my skirt I was wearing black woollen thigh-high socks (the best I could do at short notice), a black G-string (what man doesn't...?) and a black push-up bra. Hopefully, we would just skip the underwear stage. Besides, as the lyrics went, we didn't 'have to take our clothes off, to have a good time'.

Would he remember our song?

I heard a noise. My heart was beating like a crazy thing. Callum was here. Last night he called me 'darling'. Tonight I would show him what a darling I was.

The sound was coming from behind one of the huts. I listened but I knew immediately what it was. It was the unmistakable sound of people having sex. Wet hot liquid fucking. I tiptoed over. It was funny because, at first, I didn't think about it at all. I didn't think what I was doing. I didn't think what it might mean. I just marched over there in the same way I had found myself wandering around the temple in Kathmandu.

There are some things you just can't keep away from.

At first, all I could see was someone's back. Someone was kneeling on the ground and then I saw the 'M' of someone's legs looped around that back. It took me a moment to work out what was going on. I couldn't see who it was yet. Whoever was doing the servicing was doing a mind-blowingly terrific piece of work. It was absolutely spellbindingly beautiful. Bling fucking bling. I remembered seeing the same sight on the temple walls but it was better in real life. You really had to be there. I moved closer; I could see hair on the ground. I could see the receiver's shoes – orange trainers with big knots. In a moment of clarity, I knew who it was. I would have recognised those expensive-looking orange trainers anywhere. I stayed rooted to the spot. The slurping sound was incredible. I felt my stomach contract – I didn't know what it was, hate or anger, jealousy maybe. And then the sounds grew louder and louder, not just the sounds of a mouth on wetness, but sounds ranging from the deep from-the-pit-of-the-stomach groans to the God-I-can't-help-myself moans.

'Callum, you bastard!' The words didn't come out my mouth though. They stayed locked in my throat.

Well, that was certainly one way of telling someone that you aren't interested in them.

It was almost worse than the last time.

7

The next morning, as we cleared away the breakfast things, I said, 'Have a good time last night then? You and Chelle fancied doing it on the side of the mountain, did you? Or should I say, you fancied a bit of mounting on the mountain?'

I had a few minutes to spit venom at Callum because Chelle had gone to the loo. All through the curry breakfast she had been complaining, 'My stomach can't take much more of this.'

'Nice way of telling me how you feel,' I continued. 'Cheers, Callum!' Sometimes I wonder what I would have done if irony hadn't been invented. Did people really go around saying things like 'That was a horrid thing to do. You hurt me'? Still, irony or no, Callum looked like I had just told him I'd driven an axe through Chelle's head and thrown her body, complete with expensive-looking orange trainers into the lake at Pokhara.

'I don't know what you're talking about,' he mumbled.

'You liked it al fresco with me too, didn't you? Still, I thought that after the other night that you wanted us to get together again. I should have known what a rat you are. I don't know why I . . .'

'Why you what?'

'Why I still have feelings for you after all this time,' I blurted out. 'I really don't know. It's totally stupid.'

'You finished with me, remember?' he said, putting a

pile of plates down on the table. 'If you really loved me, you wouldn't have.'

Oh, that took the biscuit. Boy, I was getting angry. It was wrong, wrong, wrong. It was unjust. He was being the bloke who had had his cake and eaten it, literally, where women were concerned. When cheating went on, it was never the bloke's doing, was it? They were always the innocent party. It was always the woman's fault. Even now he was making me feel unreasonable for challenging him in the breakfast room, so early in the day. But when was the 'right' time to bring a bloke to book? No time was ever 'right'. It was infuriating. Callum was infuriating. Even last night wasn't as bad as this. In my mind I was roaring, but what actually came out was a whisper.

'I didn't *want* to finish with you, you made me,' I hissed.

'Fuck you, Lauren,' he said, and then he made this bitter sound like a laugh but more twisted. For a tiny moment I thought maybe he was pretending to be angry. I was going to say, 'I wish you *would* fuck me,' or something like that, but then he spat, he actually spat on the ground, and I knew he was deadly serious. 'Don't you remember anything?' he said, making me seem stupid.

I wanted to be swallowed up by the ground. 'Callum, why are you being like this?'

'Just fuck you!' he raged, storming out of the room as I heard the loo finally flush and Chelle bounded out.

'Oooh, that's better,' she said. 'And you've finished clearing the breakfast things away. You're learning, Lauren.'

I don't think I had ever been that cold before. And we hadn't even gone outside.

* * *

Callum and I had been together for ten months, which in teenage years (like goldfish years) is about 500 years. But it didn't feel like a long time. We had our routine but there was nothing routine about it. Each time we fucked it felt fresh. We were bonded together, peas in a pod, Adam and Eve, Hansel and Gretel, we were babes in the wood. We were fun-loving innocents. Even my parents stopped criticising us. We were left to our own devices. And our devices were loving, kissing, sucking and fucking.

In the evenings, Callum painted and I studied or, rather, I pretended to study. Really, I waited until he was ensconced in his work and then I could do no more than wait until he was ready for me again.

What I liked was kneeling as he lay down and letting him finger-fuck me as I chatted. I wasn't chatting about anything important or even anything sexy. I would just talk to him about everything that was in my mind, everything that no one else would understand. I loved talking as our fingers explored and probed. Sometimes I would have my clothes on; sometimes I would take them off. I loved watching his face: part incredulous, part lust. Then, as I felt I was near coming, I would hook myself over him, straddle him and fuck him hard.

Sometimes he would tie a dressing-gown cord around my wrists. I would lie with my arms pinned back over my head. I felt like one of those women in the silent movies; the baddies tie them up on the tracks and here, gasp, comes the steam train, choo choo. Only I was only wearing knickers and a bra, and sometimes not even that, and I had no escape. Not that I wanted to, but it was especially nice knowing that I couldn't.

Sometimes I would remind Callum: 'You do know I am completely powerless, don't you? I am under your command. I have to do what you tell me to do.' And he would come over and kneel around me, so that his cock was in my face and he would say, 'Suck it.'

After a while, I asked him if he might tie my legs up too, please, as far apart as he could. And so he did, and I made him look at me first, for what felt like hours, having him sniff all over my cunt, but never touching me, until I felt flooded there and then I would beg him for a finger or a thumb or anything. Then he would sink himself into me, and I fought against the knots for I wanted to grip his arse and pull him closer.

Sometimes we did it in the shower. We did it up against the glass. We couldn't comfortably do it standing up facing each other, as he was too tall or I was too small, so I had to turn around and stick my arse out for him. I knew he loved it like that, and I liked the way it made me feel quite dirty because it was really humiliating to stand with my bottom out, like a monkey at the zoo. But it felt great too, and sometimes I couldn't stop wailing my pleasure, and that made Callum really turned on, but he would panic too because he thought his parents might hear.

Sometimes we got back under the covers for a second time or, if we were tired out, we used to go out on his bike. On his bike it felt like we were reborn. Sometimes he would park up and we would do it in the street, standing pressed against a wall, or lying under a tree, the roots pressing on my back.

I thought nothing could go wrong.

All morning as we walked up that fucking mountain, Chelle's songs rattled around my head like a taunt. I bet she saw me last night. I bet as she was lying there getting tongued, she saw the shock on my face, and she loved it. I bet she really got off on it. 'Look, Cal, we're being watched, do me more, lick me faster.'

Even Raj joined in with Chelle's rhymes now and although I tried to rally a dissent group, the anti-song contingent, it didn't catch on. Everyone loved Chelle's pink pyjamas, her yippee, yippee, aye. They cared about the fat sausages sizzling in the pan. Eventually, though, even Chelle got bored with the sound.

'They'll play this at my funeral,' Chelle said after a particularly uninspiring chorus of 'Old Macdonald'.

I hope it's soon, I thought.

I hovered at the back, seething, watching Callum march the trail with her. I kept my eyes fixed on them. Couldn't he feel me burning a hole in his back?

Stella hung back to be with me and we marched along silently. Stones crunched beneath Chelle's feet and sometimes tumbled down towards me and Stella. I bet Chelle did it on purpose. Occasionally she or Callum paused to admire something, a wildflower or insect, maybe. Ahead lay the white-capped mountains we were all there to see. They were magnificent, but I was distracted by Chelle's backside swaying in front of me like a baby elephant. Did Callum actually like her big fat arse? I bet he cupped her buttocks at night, massaging away the pain of walking ten kilometres a day. That was when he wasn't licking her pussy behind the huts. That was when he wasn't making her scream out in pleasure in front of his ex. An insect had bitten Chelle; a trickle of blood faintly dribbled down her calf. I wondered if it could be a mosquito. Perhaps she would go down with malaria, leaving me to console Callum three or four times a day. But Chelle was as sturdy and bossy as ever.

'What's the matter, girls? You're both so slow today!' She was like a teacher, the stupid PE/geography teacher who wouldn't take no for an answer.

'Won't she fuck off?' I muttered to Stella. Stella just

grunted. It was true; Stella was particularly sluggish that morning. I didn't know what was the matter with her. I had good reason to be tired and miserable but Stella didn't. 'She's a megalomaniac,' I added.

'Oh, Chelle means well.'

'She is good at being mean, that's for sure,' I said. 'How can Callum put up with her? He deserves someone nicer.'

'Someone like you, I suppose?' Stella must have been in a foul mood for she didn't even smile at her own joke.

'Exactly,' I said, uncertain of what the best response might be.

'Come on, you slow coaches,' Chelle bleated. She was doing stretching exercises now: touch toes and bendy knees. 'You know what they say – 'no pain equals no gain!'

When we eventually caught up with her, Chelle said, 'It's more of a hike than a trek, isn't it? I expected it would be harder.'

'Well, it's not like you're carrying anything, is it?'

The young porter who was struggling under all our rucksacks and supplies raised his eyebrows at me. He definitely *was* up for it, I decided. I rationed him one smile a day. I didn't want him to grow complacent.

Even though it must have made the walk twice as hard for both of them, Callum and Chelle insisted on holding hands. It made me furious. As we climbed higher up the mountain I replayed what I had seen the night before. And what I hadn't seen, I imagined: I pictured the valley of her wide legs. I pictured the expanse of his back, the back of his head and his face as he came up for air. Chelle looked back at me plenty of times but Callum never turned around.

My footsteps seemed to beat to the rhythm of *what*

are you doing here? My sense of rejection had amplified a thousand times and now loomed all around me day and night. Hey, I thought to myself. This is probably how Elizabeth the First felt. I decided I would prefer to be the pox-ridden strumpet. At least she would have had some mates.

After lunch I went behind the bushes to pee; the young porter crept up on me from behind and tried to kiss me but he smelled of rolled tobacco and I pushed him away. I couldn't be bothered to go through with it. He was only a boy. He was probably a virgin. I wasn't aroused or even particularly flattered. Callum may have blown me out, Callum may have humiliated me again, but I wasn't *totally* desperate. I wasn't going to go with just anyone to cheer myself up.

But just before we reached the tea house that evening, the young porter tripped. I didn't see what happened, I just heard the clatter of stones and a yelp, a bit like the cry of the goats we had passed by earlier. Then the porter appeared, very sheepish. The fall had evidently knocked his childish confidence. For the first time, I thought he seemed quite likeable.

'It is my first time to have such an accident,' he said. 'I am ashamed.' Raj explained he had sprained his ankle. At dinner that evening there was a conference. Chelle was concerned that he would slow down the group.

'For his own sake,' she kept saying (so that you knew it wasn't for his sake at all!), 'he should go down.'

But Raj said he should stay. Stella did the negotiations. 'The young porter has to stay with us because he is very loyal,' she explained. 'Loyalty is a very important word to the Nepalese. He has started this work and now he would see it through.'

'Loyalty is not such an important word for us English,

is it?' I said, and I kept my eyes fixed on Callum. 'Not these days anyway.'

'I'm the sensitive type,' interrupted Chelle irrelevantly, 'I can tell that it's very important to him to feel like he's not letting the group down. However, he still has to go, otherwise he'll let us down more. Stuff the loyalty issue. '

'Oh, Callum feels the same way, don't you? Stuff loyalty!' I said. I couldn't help it. Chelle wasn't the only bitch on the mountain.

'I don't have to listen to this,' Callum shouted suddenly and it was so unusual for Callum to raise his voice that everyone turned to look at him. He stomped away from the table. I could hear him coughing behind the hut doors a few seconds later. I'm sure he regretted it the instant that he did it for if there was anything Callum hated it was being the centre of attention in that way.

Chelle didn't go after him straight away. She seemed to think it was all very funny. In fact, she punched me in the shoulder; 'Come on, you old misery. If you think this is bad, imagine how it'd be up there on Everest.'

I thought how peaceful it would be, no, how wonderful it would be, to be anywhere in the world where she wasn't.

8

When the young porter hobbled into my room that night I was quite torn. On the one hand, I really wasn't interested. I think I had forgotten how to do sex anyway, it had been that long, but on the other hand, at this stage, it would be a little, shall we say, complicated to turn him down. And I did feel sorry for him. Not as sorry as he seemed to feel for himself, but pretty sorry. Oh yes, and I did think it might just send a message out to Callum that I wasn't completely hung-up on him. I mean, I could get myself a life – if I wanted to. And, well, the young porter really did have the most amazing eyes. Now, he looked on the verge of tears.

'How's your leg?' I began. OK, so I was saying it to the wrong person, but still I couldn't let my scenarios go to waste. He sat on my bed and peeled up his trousers.

'It's OK.'

'Do you need a massage?' I enquired. Who *didn't* need a massage?

'Nah,' he said. He patted the bed and I sat down next to him. Straight away, almost before my bottom had hit the mattress, he had his arm around me and then he was kissing me.

It was nice, warm, wet. A little fast maybe but then why not?

Then he stood up and took off his shirt. I had thought he would be skinny but he was a big fucker underneath his clothes. I had supposed that marching up and down the mountains would take all the fat off him, but really he had plenty of muscle, plenty of beef. I had nothing to complain about.

We kissed again. It was good. I pulled away and studied his face. He shut his eyes when we kissed. Perhaps he was imagining a young girl in his hometown with braids that swung over her school books as she studied by candlelight. I shut my eyes when we kissed too.

'Are you worried about the storm?' I said, more for something to say than because I cared.

'Me? No.' He laughed. 'I'm a big boy.' Somehow that didn't give me any confidence.

He looked at me coyly. Somehow his face said, 'You really want me, don't you?' I didn't think I did, until then. But the expression worked. It really made me want him.

He was only half my age. The thought that men do it without a second thought didn't make me feel entirely better.

But it helped.

'Have you done it before?' I asked. I meant to say, 'With a foreigner?' but it seemed a little strange so I left it at that.

'Yes,' he said. 'I can give you a great pleasure.'

Well, I thought, a little pleasure would be nice.

Without delay he whipped his trousers off and lay on top of me. I pulled his buttock cheeks tight. He really had a smooth bottom, not at all hairy, very pretty. His spine protruded. I rubbed my breasts against him. He squealed and squirmed with delight. I pushed him off and got down and I pressed my face to his groin. I moved my tongue over his cock. I swiped up and down with the vigour of a checkout girl and her first tool.

'Oh yeah.'

He had a nice responsive cock but I was feeling, if not exactly bored, a little detached. Maybe he realised that for he pulled me up and then he pushed me down on to the bed. I liked the way he looked then; the dark fringe in his eyes, the smile and the surprisingly manly shoulders, so it was a little disappointing when he turned me around.

He fucked me from behind as I leaned over the bed. I chewed the sheets and then I thought, sod this, I want everyone to hear that we are fucking. I want Callum to know it and I want Chelle to know it.

I pushed my buttocks against his cock. I pressed back and he groaned as he realised he didn't have to do a thing, just hold still, stay hard and I would do the work. I would fuck him. He would go in and out of me, but it would be me making the moves. And I did. I worked him up and down me. And I grabbed his hands and put them on me. A hand on my tit and a hand on my clit. We picked up speed and I thought it was Callum, Callum was fucking me from behind, Callum was going deeper than I thought possible, Callum was whispering wet sticky words into my ear.

And then the young porter surged forwards and the movement of his cock grew faster and faster and I couldn't stop myself and I felt the powerful jerk of his orgasm and yet I worked it, worked it, wouldn't let it go until I had come as well.

'What will your boss say?' I said, thinking of Raj, and how he didn't seem keen on fraternising with the trekkers.

The porter shook his arrogant head.

'He's not my boss.'

'He's not?'

'Nah, I'm his boss.'

I thought he was joking. That annoyed him. 'Raj is

not a real guide,' he persisted, getting cross. He kicked the floor and then belatedly realised that his leg was hurting. He winced with pain. It made me giggle a little. 'Raj is from the south. It's his first time up the mountains. He wants the money.'

'Is it your first time too?'

I wondered how I could get the young porter to leave me alone. I had had what I wanted. It was great but it wasn't brilliant. And poor Stella. I had no doubt she was waiting patiently in the dining room for us to finish.

The young porter thought my question was very funny. 'You think I'm a baby, don't you?'

I was crueler than I knew. 'Well, aren't you?'

'You didn't think that a minute ago,' he said triumphantly. 'When I made you come!'

You didn't make me come, I thought. *I* did. Don't confuse the two.

'I only did this because I feel sorry for you.'

'You! You pity me!' He couldn't believe it. 'You were desperate for it!'

'I was only pretending,' I said. I knew that would get him out of here. I rolled on to my stomach and acted as though I was getting ready to sleep. 'You weren't bad for a kid but...'

'I'm not a child!' He was nearly howling. 'I'll show you!'

'Yeah,' I said mockingly. 'Right!'

He lifted me up. There are fireman's lifts and there are porter's lifts. I now know which one is worse. In a second, and in one swift move, I was yanked upside down so the blood rushed to my head and my arms were locked, impotent, against him. If I kicked him I was afraid I would smash head-first on to the floor.

He walked me, like this, outside. I was still laughing, part crying. This couldn't be happening.

'Put me down! C'mon, I was only joking.'

'I'll show you,' he kept saying to my ankles. 'I am not a child!'

I realised that I didn't have a hope in hell of beating him off. I just hoped he wouldn't drop me.

He carried me like that for about a minute and then restored me the right way up. I was dizzy and I had to cling on to him to stop myself from falling down.

'Look!' he said proudly.

I looked and when I saw I gripped him tighter. 'For fuck's sake, what are you doing?'

He had brought us to a ledge, a tiny offshoot out from the edge of the cliff. There was barely any land behind us. The worst thing was, there was none in front of us.

'I'm going to show you I'm not a kid,'

'Not here.'

'Yes.'

I was too scared to hit him. If he fell he would take me down with him.

'Put me back,' I said. 'Take me back, right now … and we'll –' I tried to remember what my teachers used to say '– we'll forget all about this.'

'I'm going to make you come,' he said. That foolish, arrogant little shit. I was petrified. I told him that I would scream.

'No one will come,' he laughed, 'except you.'

'Help me,' I said. I guess that was the moment I realised I didn't even know his name.

He held me tight. I could feel his hard-on pressing on my thigh.

'Don't hurt me,' I pleaded.

'I'm going to fuck you,' he explained, 'here.'

I did something stupid. I looked down and it must have been miles and miles drop beneath us. 'Please …'

I sighed. I didn't know whether I should shut my eyes or not. There's that theory that shutting your eyes is worse because what you imagine is often worse than the reality. I can assure you that here the reality was worse than anything I could imagine. 'Help me!' I prayed. 'Please God.'

I don't know what God was doing, but the young porter parted my legs and inserted his cock. He fucked me on the cliff edge, very slowly and very gently. His cock slid up and down me as I stood frozen in fear. I could feel the pressure in my clit. I couldn't move a muscle. I couldn't even breathe. But I could shout and shout I did. I shouted with fear and then with pleasure, and then I told everyone on the mountain that I was coming. I'm sure my voice flew out, over towards the villages, and over to the city. I'm sure my cries must have woken people from their dreams or their night-mares; I'm sure everyone heard. I had never been so terrified or so turned on in all my life.

At breakfast, the young porter cooked me an especially thick slice of toast. The others looked at me resentfully.

'How did you sleep?' I asked Chelle, smiling. I was sure she was going to moan about the terrible racket in the night. She was very insistent on getting her seven hours beauty sleep. (Much good it did her!)

'Wonderfully,' she said. 'I always do. Like a log.'

Like a plank, I thought. I had gone to all that effort and she had been out for the count. Great!

9

Snow fell. As we walked, little flakes landed on our fingers. The cold bit into our noses. The mountains looked magic. I couldn't stop laughing to myself as I remembered what had happened the previous night. The young porter made a walking stick out of a branch and, for once, I rather enjoyed his company. He was surprisingly easy to talk to. He didn't apologise for frightening the life out of me but then I didn't apologise for being such a bitch. There was none of that 'the-day-after' embarrassment between us. It seemed, as far as he was concerned, the sex, even hanging-off-a-cliff sex, was all part of the service. He talked a little about a girlfriend. When I asked if she was jealous, he looked surprised and said, 'What of?' Then he asked if anyone had my heart. I said maybe and he grinned like he knew.

I was certainly in love. I was in love with the mountains.

In the late afternoon, we arrived at a little tin cabin where Raj said we would spend the night. There was nobody there and there was very little furniture or anything left. It looked like everyone had left in a hurry taking everything with them.

'All the people have gone south,' Raj explained. 'The porters, the cooks, everyone has gone.'

'It is getting colder,' the young porter agreed. 'The season is nearly over.'

I remembered something we used to learn at school.

It was from the Bible I think. I didn't usually pay attention – the Bible was too full of 'should' and 'should not' to fit my world, but this had appealed to me: there are seasons to laugh, seasons to cry, seasons to love, seasons to hate. I looked at Callum as he entered the room. He seemed fazed. I don't know if it was the emptiness of the place or that we had finally stopped moving.

There are seasons to fuck. There are seasons to be fucked.

Callum slumped into a chair. Sometimes the tiredness didn't hit you until you stopped.

'We have to get organised,' Chelle said. 'Lauren, why don't you tidy up the cabin?'

'What did your last slave die of?' I muttered. Stella gave me her best peacemaker's look. Chelle organised the others into groups. One group would go and look for wood. The others (oh, how convenient she put herself on the easiest task!) would catch chickens. Callum, who was shivering like a blancmange, asked nervously if he might possibly wait behind. Chelle gave him special dispensation. You would think she was the pope or something.

As soon as they left, Callum leaned towards me. I knew he was going to say something 'about us' and, although I desperately wanted to be alone with him, I have to admit I was a bit worried. We hadn't spoken since our major row the day before, but it wasn't that that perturbed me but that his teeth wouldn't stop knocking against each other; the sound they made was pretty ghoulish. And he seemed to be having trouble catching his breath.

'Are you OK, Callum?' I said. 'You're looking a bit under the weather.'

Under the weather? It was the understatement of the century.

'Lauren,' Callum said, like he had been waiting to do this for some time. He took hold of my hands. His were freezing. His chest was going up and down really quickly. I wanted to think it was the effect I was having on him, but I knew that probably wasn't true. 'I'm so sorry about the other night.'

'It's OK. I understand. After all, she is your wife!'

Callum looked at me a little strangely.

'Yeah, well, I know you're under stress but I was just a bit surprised at your reaction.'

I'm under stress? I thought. Still, I let it go. 'What do you want to say to me, Callum?'

'You know nothing's going to happen between us, don't you?'

Did he have to launch in with the bad news straight away? Would there be no I-love-you preliminary, no but-you're-so-special small talk?

'Yes,' I admitted. 'I think I know that by now. But I can't stop thinking about it; about you. I want to be with you.'

'Be with me?'

Well, he asked for it. 'I want to fuck you.'

He winced. I didn't know if it was the words he hated or the idea.

'Don't say it.'

'I can't help it. I want to fuck your brains out. I don't know what it is. I don't know if it's being here in this place after dreaming of it for so long, I don't know if it's because of our past, but I've never felt this way before. All I can think of is your cock and having it inside me and coming on top of you and underneath you, and having you –'

'Stop,' Callum said. 'Please stop. I would love it too, babe, you know that, but I can't. My life is with Chelle now.'

'But don't you just wonder how it would feel if you just unzipped your trousers and pulled out your cock and put it between my thighs? And then if you moved it higher and put it in me? Don't you wonder how it would feel?'

'Christ!' he said through gritted teeth. 'I want to fuck you so badly, I can't think about anything else. You know every step I take up this goddamn mountain I'm thinking about you. I'm thinking about kissing your beautiful throat, squeezing your horny big tits, about getting inside your lovely wet crack.'

I moved nearer to him. I had to be careful. I had to be cautious, as if he were an unfamiliar cat that I didn't want to frighten away.

'I'll be so wet for you, Callum. I want to see your face as you pump your cock into me, and I want to call out your name as you come inside me.'

Just as I thought he was going to kiss me, the door opened.

'I spy,' I said loudly, as the wind blew the others in laughing, 'with my little eye . . .' Callum had a hard-on, I was sure of it. I saw the outline pushing against his trousers. I think we could safely call it a 'generous' size.

'Fantastic news,' Chelle said. 'Raj said we could go to base camp if we want.'

'Something beginning with S?'

Shit. Shit. Shit. Who gave a fuck about base camp? I couldn't even get to first base with Callum.

Stella saw my expression and, being Ms Diplomacy, she produced a compromise. 'Let's decide tomorrow.'

Callum was leaning against the table; the table was supporting him, I think. For once, he ignored Chelle. He was just looking directly at me and I could see the lust in his eyes, but I could see something else.

He shook his head and mouthed it: 'Sorry, I can't.'

I thought about throwing myself off the side of the mountain but I wouldn't want to give that witch the satisfaction.

Her last slave probably committed suicide.

Dinner was a subdued affair – or was that just me? We didn't heat up the food for long enough, so it tasted luke-warm even though somehow the top layer of everything was burnt.

'Rice again?' I said. As soon as the words were out of my mouth I knew I shouldn't have said anything. Chelle wouldn't waste any opportunity to score points.

'This isn't the Ritz, Lauren. If you wanted a luxury holiday you shouldn't have come.'

After the soup, Callum left the table. He whispered that he needed to lie down. A few minutes later, Chelle got up.

'Excuse me, everyone,' she smirked, 'honeymoon calls.'

Stella asked me if I wanted to look at her photos from Kathmandu. She had got them developed when she was there but had forgotten to show them to me. I shuffled through the pictures greedily. Stella wasn't the best photographer but she took so many shots that some of them couldn't help but turn out great.

There were way too many shots of Chelle at one or other stupid Stupa. Then there was Chelle by a sandwich stand, Chelle in front of an ox, Chelle eating ice cream. There was only a couple of Stella. In one she and Chelle had their arms around each other. In another, Chelle had done rabbit's ears over Stella's head.

There was one of Callum and me as we returned from the river that first day. We were blurry. Stella must have been focusing on the temple behind us, but we were there too, standing too far apart. You couldn't call us friends; it was the 'hey-there's-nothing going-on-here' way that exes pose.

In another photo Callum was sitting on a wall, wiping his hand across his forehead. I was in that picture too. I was in profile and I was looking at him. I can't remember when it was taken. I don't think I knew. I was looking at him the way hungry children peer in baker-shop windows in sentimental old-fashioned movies.

'Are you feeling sad?' Stella said. 'You wish you were with him, don't you?'

I didn't want to see any more photos. This wasn't doing me any good.

'It's all right,' I said magnanimously. 'I'm fine.'

'I wonder if there is anything I can do to make you feel better.' Stella said it so softly that I wasn't sure that she actually had. Then, when I didn't reply, she added, 'You're so beautiful. Callum must be mad to, you know, to not want to be with you.'

'Do you really think so?'

'Yes. Any man ... or woman would give their right arm to sleep with you, Lauren.'

I wriggled in my sleeping bag. I waited until I felt sure what she meant. She did mean that, didn't she?

'Look, Stella, that's really kind of you but I'm not a...'

'Not a what?'

'A you know what.'

Stella smiled. 'You don't have to be a you know what to let me help you feel a bit better.'

I thought of what Callum and Chelle were doing now. The 'honeymoon calls'. I bet she had him fucking her all night long. I bet she made him lick her cunt until his tongue fell off. I bet they didn't think of me.

Stella, on the other hand, seemed to have my best

interest right at heart. (Or some other part of her anatomy.)

'You really think I'm ... beautiful, huh?'

'You know you are, Lauren.'

'Would you like to touch me?' My voice sounded like it belonged to someone else.

'I would like to touch you very much.'

There, I had my answer.

'Where would you like to touch me?'

'Here, in the hut.'

'No, I mean where on my body?'

Stella had a tremor in her voice. She must have felt shy too. 'I would like to touch your breasts ...' Stella then added 'first'. 'I would like to touch your breasts *first*.' She wasn't missing a trick. This is the girl I had thought never had a sexual thought in her life!

So I pulled up my top. It felt very strange, like being in the doctor's or something. I lay down and Stella laughed and I realised that it was me who was the nervous one; she wasn't anxious at all.

'Shall I take off your bra or will you?'

I said I would but, cack-handed, it seemed to take forever to undo the clasp. Then it fell down on my lap and I lay down awkwardly again.

'Relax, Lauren,' Stella said and then she leaned over me and before I could say, 'It's impossible to relax' or 'I've never done this before' my nipple was in her mouth and she was flickering over it in a movement that was so wonderful I could feel the creamy sensation in my knickers.

'Oh, yes,' I said, and I felt silly saying it so soon but it really was an 'oh yes' moment. And she got right down to my chest and squeezed my tits together and had them both in her fantastic mouth at the same time, and she was doing that thing with her tongue. I couldn't believe she was doing it and I couldn't believe I was not only letting her but encouraging her.

I bent my knees and parted my legs and I think I made it obvious that, yes, she was welcome down there too, at least her fingers were, but she was in no hurry; she took her time. She teased my breasts like she was born to it. Maybe she was.

I remembered what she said to me that time: 'The first time can be quite an experience!' Well, she was right about that.

Finally, I undid my trousers and she smiled at me. 'You're impatient.'

'Sorry,' I said. I felt ashamed; maybe women didn't do this kind of thing, but Stella shook her head. She grinned. It didn't matter. Everything I did was fine by her. And, as I lay there, receiving those beautiful licks and sucks on my tits, I felt a little guilty. Did she want me to do the same to her? I didn't want to. No matter how guilty I felt, it wasn't enough to raise myself out of this soft feeling and do anything. It was too relaxing. It was so gooood. After what seemed like a very long time, I heard Stella's voice from around my waist.

'Now I'm going to put a finger inside you, is that OK?'

'Uh huh.'

'Say it properly.'

'What?'

'Say what you want me to do.'

'I want you to put a finger up me.'

'Say my name.'

'Stella.'

'I mean, say it all together.'

'I want you to put a finger up me, Stella.'

'Anything else?'

'I want you to rub me, Stella. Oh, Christ, that's it!'

Her fingers were at my hole and then she had inserted one then two then maybe, I'm not sure, three fingers. She was so soft but so nimble. She knew exactly what she was doing and if she doubted it, she would stare me in the face and say, 'Like this, Lauren? Or ...' And I would say, 'Oh, fuck, yeah, that's it, like that, don't stop.'

I started to squirm and push against her fingers. I rocked back and forth. My bottom was up in the air, supported by my legs. My slippery slit was in her line of vision. So this is what is meant by a bird's-eye view.

'Please, please, don't stop, Stella.'

'Anything else?'

I knew what else she was angling for but I couldn't bring myself to say it. Yes, I was turned on but I didn't want her long hair tickling the insides of my thighs. I didn't want her feminine chin rubbing my wet cunt. The only people who get to do that are male. A girl has to have some boundaries. Finally, she asked me straight out: 'Do you want me to lick you too?'

'No,' I said, and she accepted that, although I suppose my heart did sink when she didn't put up any resistance at all.

The pressure in my pussy was unbelievable, however. She knew more about what turned me on than I did. I rocked into her, fucking her fingers. She gave just the right amount of stimulation and when she could feel me getting there, when she could feel the tension mount, she bent her head and nibbled expertly at my nipples.

'I want to come. Oh, Christ, Stella, let me come.'

And she was up close and telling me it was OK. She said, 'Let go, darling, let it all out, you deserve it. You've been so patient. It's OK, just enjoy. Let it out.'

'Oh, fuck me, fuck me, Stella.' I screamed and I urged the fingers inside me. 'Callum, Callum, Callum.'

I felt the orgasm rush through my body. I cried out and pulled Stella close to me. She fell on my chest; my tits were in her mouth. Her hair was like silk sheets in my hands.

I wasn't used to silk sheets. I was a cotton girl really.

After that, it seemed silly to keep secrets from her, so I told Stella what had happened between Callum and me. I told her that Callum and I had made a plan to meet but then he had been there with Chelle. I told her that, despite the darkness, I knew exactly what was going on.

Stella listened very carefully. I had never known anyone to listen the way she did. It was like she was listening to the very core of what you said. It made me pick my words more carefully than usual. 'I just ... it hurt me so much. He said he'd be there *for me* and then he was out there fucking, or rather sucking, her.'

When I had finished Stella said, 'Are you sure it was him?'

'What do you mean?'

'You saw them? You actually saw them both?'

'Yes,' I reconsidered. 'Well, I definitely saw her.'

'It couldn't have been someone else with her? When was this? Two nights ago you say?'

'Someone else with her? No way. I mean, they *are* on honeymoon. He set it up. He said he would be out there and, yes, he was. I just didn't expect him to be out there with his face in her pussy. He did it to get to me. God knows why!'

'Why are you so convinced of that?'

'Because of last time,' I said. 'Because of what happened then.'

One word. No, two: Rose Connelly.

* * * *

Callum's mate Dave had the greenest eyes you've ever seen. He thought having beautiful eyes made him special. You could tell he thought he was a charmer. I didn't. I saw right through him. Green eyes or not. As far as I was concerned, Callum and Dave weren't real friends, they had just worked with each other 'on the decks' as they called it, and had carried on, out of habit, doing the same things together.

I wasn't to be jealous; even back then I knew I couldn't be all things to Callum. I could be his girl, his lover, his best friend, but I couldn't be a casual mate down the pub. I couldn't be the guy who he went with to the footie. I couldn't make stupid jokes.

I found it hard when we went to O'Harts. Callum and I were better at the beach or lying down in his or my bedroom. At O'Harts, Dave was always there, getting between us tearing up cigarette packets and matchboxes. They would be ripped into pieces by the end of the night. Or he lit matches and let them burn out in the ashtray. Dave had girlfriends but he never talked to them when he was out drinking and he disapproved of Callum for letting me come along.

The sad thing was I really wanted Dave to like me. He screwed all the girls, any girls, and I didn't know why but he showed absolutely no interest in me. I'm not saying I *wanted* him to fancy me, but a flicker of interest, like he gave everyone else, would have been good. Once, on the way home, I saw Dave in someone's garden. His trousers were round his ankles and I could see his white buttocks going up and down. I couldn't see the girl at all, she was in the shadows, so I've no idea who it was; I couldn't even be certain it was him, but I knew it was; I could see the way his buttocks heaved in and out and it was mesmerising.

Callum had only known Dave for a few months but,

if you didn't know, you might have thought they were born in adjacent hospital beds, so far back did their friendship seem to go.

Once, when we were in the pub, Callum went to put a song on the jukebox. I remember that the song Callum liked at the time was 'Solid as a Rock' and sometimes I would whisper 'Solid as your cock' in his ear. But I remember that time not because of the song but because I was left alone with Dave and his matches. He lit one, but this time he didn't let it go. I watched the flame creep up the stick towards his fingers. I waited for him to drop it.

'What do you think about Callum and Rose, eh?'

'What's there to think?'

Rose Connelly was an orange girl with an over-bite and, when she wasn't at O'Harts, she worked at a tanning salon.

'They're fucking.' Finally, Dave dropped the match into the ashtray where it continued to smoulder.

'Fucking? Who?'

'Each other, you twat. Rose and Callum are fucking.'

He said this whenever we were alone together, I suppose. Another time, when Callum was at the bar, Dave whispered to me, 'Talked to him about Rose yet?'

Callum always bought many more rounds than Dave did, even though it was Dave who worked in the city and, as he put it, 'earned the shedloads of cash.'

'There's nothing to say. I trust him completely.'

Dave laughed.

'It was someone else with Chelle,' Stella said abruptly.

'The porter, you mean? No, I don't think so. I know what he's like.'

'Umm, guess again.'

'I don't know. It *was* Callum. I'm sure of it.'

Now I thought about it, I didn't know what I remembered and what I had imagined. The only thing I had seen for certain in the darkness was the orange shoes and the legs.

'You're not the only woman who is ... um ... not officially a lesbian, you know.'

'Not you?' I said. Not you, not you.

The idea wasn't able to go in, but seemed to bounce off the surface of my brain. Not Stella; Stella didn't have sex. She wasn't that kind of girl. But then I thought about all the times I had interrupted Chelle and Stella in one of their huddles. And the time I found Stella further up the mountain path and she was defensive and nervous; had I interrupted them having sex?

'Oh, but how? When? When did it start?'

'The first night.'

'The first night?'

'You remember we lost you? Well, she did it on purpose.'

'No way!'

'We were walking back. She just grabbed me and kissed me. I couldn't believe she was so forward actually. She put her tongue in my mouth and then when we were ... when we were holding each other, she gave me a lovebite. I was really afraid you would see it.'

I remembered the flowery tablecloth that Stella wore around her neck. So that's what it was about!

'And?'

'The next day we went to the temple; yes, don't look so shocked, Lauren. Chelle is not as dull as you think.'

'And do you like her?'

Stella shrugged. 'She's OK.'

'Do you like her? I mean, do you like her more than me?'

I thought she would scold me. I thought she would

say something like 'Don't compare, Lauren,' or 'You're being silly now,' but instead she said, 'I like you more.' And then she got on top of me and kissed me ferociously.

I hadn't finished with the questions though.

'So what did you do with Chelle?'

This changed everything.

'I can do it to you if you like. I'll show you what we did,' Stella offered. She kissed me again. She sucked my lips.

'Do it to me,' I said. 'Do what you did to her.'

I was thinking, fuck you, Chelle. You might have Callum by the balls, but you haven't got Stella. You think you've got your cake and you're eating it – but hey, babe, *I've* got your cake and I'm eating it too.

Or rather Stella was.

Stella had parted my legs. I felt her look at me. Only when she was right down there, gazing at me, did I dare ask, 'Is my pussy better than hers?'

'It's the most beautiful thing I've ever seen. Forget the mountains. This is the best view in the world. Do you really want me to do what I did to Chelle?'

I said, 'Yes, yes.' I did. Why not? I was ready and if it was good enough for that stupid cow then it was good enough for me. So, this time, Stella didn't just use her fingers on me but she licked me there as well. She went right down to my pubic hair and spread me apart and she slipped her tongue along my cunt before dunking it, teasing it inside me.

'Is it OK?' she murmured, but she kept working it. She didn't need an answer and every few seconds she had to come up for air and she gave this delicious sighing noise as she went back down again into all that creamy stickiness. And she seemed to really love doing it; she couldn't get enough of it; she manoeuvred herself so that she had more, more of me on her tongue and in her mouth. I couldn't stop pushing, jerking against her. I felt my excitement grow at the same time as hers so that I rubbed against her and jiggled more. She used her fingers too, doing fucking moves, in and out, but she didn't let up the long wet strokes with her tongue.

And then, when I was close to crying out, she got her hairbrush from the bedside table and very gently, but very firmly, she held my thighs apart and she slid it into me. She was still there though, still licking around that whole area. I could feel her eyes on me. She fucked me with the arm of the brush and then – I'm assuming she did the same to Chelle – she made me suck on her finger. Even as I did it I was thinking, uh oh, what's she playing at? But I did it anyway, I was too far gone to resist, and then I felt it come round, up behind me. She spread my buttock cheeks and found that small small puckered hole.

I said no, but she said, 'I did this to Chelle; don't you want me to do the same?'

And I did, but I didn't want to have to say it, but she knew anyway and anyhow, she knew I loved it dirty and earthy even before I did. The brush stayed up my slit, her finger was pushing at my arsehole and then, once again, she bent low and she drank in my tits and I was lost, railing and rocking against it all.

'Oh, don't stop, yes, that's it, yes, that's it, Cal-*lum*!'

'Can I see the rest of the photos?' I asked Stella when I had come back down to earth. I didn't think they would hurt me in the same way now.

Stella looked happy but serious at the same time.

'Lauren,' she said, 'be careful with Chelle.'

'Why? Did you tell her how I feel about Callum?'

Stella turned away so I couldn't see her face, but I

could tell from her voice that I had hurt her. 'I wouldn't tell your secrets, Lauren,' she said. 'But it wouldn't take much for Chelle to work it out.'

I couldn't sleep. I tried to talk myself into it since I was worried about being too tired to walk the next day, but that made it worse. I tried to tell myself that three hours' sleep was adequate. I shouldn't sweat about it; after all, three hours is better than nothing. But really I knew, it wasn't enough. It *really* wasn't enough.

I kept going over what Stella and I had done. I would never have dreamed that she would do such things, or that I would respond in that way. I wondered if I was as keen on Callam as I had first thought. Perhaps my loathing of Chelle was fuelling my passion in order to make a point. That I was better than her, or some kind of immature rivalry. I wanted to wake Stella up and discuss it. No, who was I kidding? I wanted to wake her up so she could go me again – and faster and harder this time. I was ready for her now!

It felt like it was still the middle of the night when I heard the call of the morning birds.

10

'Callum is sick.' The way Chelle said it as she burst into our hut just after sunrise suggested that it was an inconvenience more than anything else.

I think Stella must have been pretending to be asleep because there was no way you could possibly sleep through Chelle. Chelle leaped on to my bed and she wrapped up in my blanket, mulling over the dilemma. The porters brought us hot chai. My young porter winked at me. 'Good night?' he asked.

'Good morning,' I said sternly, but I couldn't stop grinning. I felt on top of the world. Of course Callum was sick. He would have to be to put up with Chelle. I didn't care anymore. The previous day, the young porter had taught me some Nepalese, and I used it now. I said that something smelt like 3-day old goat's eye soup. Chelle must have realised I wasn't being entirely friendly.

I then added a deft little phrase that translates as 'I love an erection as big as Everest'. The young porter fell to the floor, coughing. Chelle scowled.

'Why does it always happen to me?' Chelle asked. She didn't seem to expect an answer. 'I suppose its altitude sickness or something.'

I wanted to say that it wasn't exactly happening to her, but I felt guilty enough as it was. Maybe I had brought it on them; I had been wishing so hard that Chelle would get sick, or collapse over the mountain edge, that I couldn't help thinking that maybe the gods had been listening after all but had misheard the name.

Stella got up. She looked terrible. Her hair was all mussed up. It reminded me that her hair brush was at the bottom of my bed.

'Are you sick too?' Chelle asked.

'I'm OK,' Stella said. 'I didn't sleep much.'

'Were you cold?'

'Cold? No it wasn't that.'

'Callum's not well,' I said quickly.

'I'm not surprised,' Stella said. 'He's been looking peaky for days.'

'I don't know what to do,' Chelle whined.

'You don't have a choice, do you?' I really felt like shaking her sometimes. 'If he has got altitude sickness, the only solution is to take him down lower, where the air isn't so thin, where he can breathe easily again. And with the storm coming maybe we all should.'

'But it's so fantastic here.' Chelle looked around contentedly. 'And I think Raj has got it wrong about all that too. I spoke to one trekker before we came and she said the guides always make these things up so that they can get off home early.'

Outside the hut the porters were making rice and smoking roll-ups. Chelle borrowed my mirror. She pouted at her reflection. She really *did* fancy herself.

'I'm not much good at the Florence Nightingale stuff,' she said. 'It's really not my thing.'

I knew that Chelle didn't want to go down. I read once that the prerequisite for happiness was good health, stupidity and selfishness; Chelle had these three by the bucketload. And Chelle had decided that she would do the Himalayas and it would take more than Callum's illness to stop her.

* * *

After breakfast, I stood with the young porter and we gazed into the mountain range. 'Fantastic!' I said.

And he said, 'But you know there are wolves and bears and all sorts of dangerous creatures out there.'

I said, 'I know that,' and we both laughed.

The mountains didn't look real that morning. They looked like something you get on a tea towel or on a keyring. They were just too white. The sky was just too blue. It was picture-perfect. I told the young porter that Callum was ill and he said he would go and check on him. A few minutes later, he stalked out of Chelle and Callum's hut; his limp was evidently forgotten in the excitement. He was a mixture of fury and self-importance.

'That man is *very* sick. He must go down lower now.'

Chelle followed me out on to the path. I knew she was there but I ignored her until finally she pulled at my arm. She had covered up the extent of Callum's sickness, just so that we would keep going. If anything, she was the sick one.

'I know you want to take Callum down,' she began.

'What?' I couldn't believe it. 'I think we should *all* take him down. We came up as a group and we should go down as a group.'

'There's no point doing that,' she said. 'We paid a fortune for this and I'll be damned if I don't get to see base camp now. But I know you don't care and I know something else. You would be quite happy to go back with Callum.'

I hadn't expected that. I didn't know I was so transparent. Was it Stella? Had Stella told her how I felt?

'What do you mean?' I asked, amazed that my voice didn't sound as unsteady as it felt. 'Why would I want to do that?'

'It's obvious,' she sighed. 'You're always looking at us.'

'That's not true.' I felt desperate. I just didn't want it to come out like this. I felt like I had been caught doing something silly.

Chelle sat down on a rock and drew circles in the dust with her feet. God, I hated her shoes. Those god-damn trainers were nothing but trouble. She looked up at me coyly.

'You find me attractive, don't you?'

'I ... er ... no!'

'You're not really my type, Lauren, I think you know that deep down, but if you really did look after Callum for a couple of days then I would certainly consider doing something for you.'

That vain cow! She thought I was interested in *her*. She really thought I was in love with her, not Callum!

'Uh ...' I couldn't think of what to say.

'You're really a sweet girl. And that really would impress me. I'm sure I could make it worth your while.'

Chelle put her hand on her breast and started very slowly playing with her nipple. I couldn't stop staring but not for the reason she seemed to think. Was she really trying to seduce me into taking Callum down the mountain?

'Er,' I said, 'I will take him if that's what you want.'

'I do,' she said. 'There aren't many people in the world I can trust, but you're someone I can. And, well, it's a little difficult now, under the circumstance, but I will thank you *properly* when we get back.'

'No, no, there's no need.'

'I absolutely insist, Lauren.' She came up very close to me and stared me deeply in the eyes. She tilted her head very slightly and I thought she was going to kiss me but she didn't. She was just teasing me. Then she poked her tongue out, ever so slightly, and closed her eyes.

When her eyes were shut I quickly managed to take a step back.

'So you'll do it then?' she said. 'You'll leave now. You can take two men and some food. You won't need much.'

Somehow it had been decided.

'You really trust me with Callum, do you?' I asked and I laughed as if it were a great joke.

'Oh yes. Callum wouldn't do unfaithful and he certainly wouldn't be unfaithful to me.'

I thought, you don't know Rose Connelly and you don't really know me.

Another time. We were in Dave's car on the way home from O'Harts. Dave stopped at the petrol station. He told Callum to go pay. Callum winced but did it anyway. Dave wasn't wearing his seat belt. He turned around and leaned right into me in the back. I was wearing the new diamanté earrings that Callum had given me, a miniskirt and new black strappy sandals. I had dressed up but Dave always looked at me as if to say, 'Why the fuck do you bother?'

'You're a right mug, you are. Everyone's laughing at you.'

Was Dave especially horrid to me, I wondered, because I was younger? Dave found it funny to call me 'jail bait', 'small fry' or a zillion other names that I didn't really understand, but I could guess their meaning.

'Ask Callum. Ask him; he'll tell you. Rose Connelly. Do you want me to spell it for you?'

I didn't say anything. I stared out the window and wished Callum back quicker. Then Dave tipped me off.

'They'll be in town tomorrow,' he said smugly, like he was giving me a cert-to-win on the horses. 'Usually, they don't go public –' Dave turned the key in the ignition '– but I guess they figure everyone knows, right?'

I was allowed to choose two men out of the three to accompany Callum and myself to the lower slopes. I chose the two porters. I could see the relief on Chelle's face as she saw that I wasn't taking Raj. She couldn't believe I was taking 'Hobnob', as she now called him, and the other porter.

The three of them left to go up before we started the descent. I waved them away and as I watched Chelle's backside wobble into the distance I felt a great happiness. It was even better than waving my parents off on their annual summer holidays all those years ago.

Callum didn't wave. Callum was delirious. I don't think he could see with those rolling eyes. He was still handsome though, even with his face drenched with petals of sweat. He didn't know what was going on.

Why couldn't it have been Chelle who got sick? Callum and I could have been striding at the top of the mountain now, hand in hand. The hills could have been alive to the sound of our music. We could have been playing out scenarios one and two all day long. No, the thing was, Callum would have stopped for Chelle. He would have taken care of her. There was no question of it.

Callum groaned. I don't think he was sleeping. He was in that in and out miasma of consciousness, light and dark, noise and quiet, external and internal worlds bewilderingly colliding. Was it the beating of his heart or the porter's shuffling outside that I could hear?

'Callum?' I whispered. I pushed a rogue hair off his

forehead. His fringe dangled dark and low, ominous like a heavy cloud. 'We're going to take you down. You're going to have to be very brave.'

He took my hand. His palm was sweaty, almost greasy, but I found it torturously arousing. I could barely move for fear of giving myself away. This was not how I was supposed to feel. For the next few days I was his nurse, that's all. Yet, I locked hold of his hand, exploring his fingers. I had to take every opportunity I could. I glided down the dip between his fingers. It made me shiver a little.

'Callum, you'll be fine, I promise.'

I didn't think he could hear me, so it was a shock when he whispered, 'I'm holding you to that.'

I swear if I were an ice cream, I would have melted.

11

We walked for just two hours that first morning. The young porter hauled Callum along. They looked like soldiers in a war film – the one wounded and the other barely conscious. The other porter pulled the tents and rucksacks. Me? I just worried in between and wished I hadn't had sex with the young porter because he had started giving me meaningful looks. It wasn't until later that I realised that he wasn't looking at me in a sexual way but he was trying to console me for something – for something that hadn't happened yet.

They set up lunch underneath an overhang. I wanted to keep on going but the young porter said, 'It's dangerous to go too fast,' and he patted my hand.

It was too uncomfortable to sit. We crouched there as Callum dozed. Compared to our other meals, it was a miserable occasion. There was flat bread for them and one for Callum and me to share. We hadn't brought much of the food since we were the ones going down. Chelle, Stella and Raj had most of the supplies, but Callum wasn't eating anything anyway.

Before they left, Stella had warned me that Callum might be fitful and agonised but I hadn't taken her seriously. I suppose even at that stage I had regarded this as a game and me as the winner. See how I had played Chelle! But now I could see that Callum was in a terrible way. I can only imagine what dark dreams he was having. It was like he was away on an acid trip that had gone wrong. I couldn't bring him round. I tried to shake him but there was nothing. When I realised the young porter was still staring at me with sympathy, I began to grow nervous. Still, I thought, how long could it possibly take us to get down?

That afternoon we had only walked two hours more when they said it was time to stop. We would set up the tents and spend the night here. Again, it seemed to me they were giving up too soon.

'We have to go on,' I said. I couldn't help feeling that if I were Chelle they would have; it was just because it was me that they were being cheeky. I offered to take hold of the supplies to give one of them a break. I pleaded with them but they said, 'It is safer to go slower,' and then finally they told me to look at Callum.

'For Christ's sake, I know what Callum looks like.' Actually, I felt like his image was printed on the inside of my eyelids.

'Look closely.'

So I did, and then I saw what they saw. Poor Callum. His eyes were rolling. For the first time I felt really scared and I also felt the weight of responsibility. I had taken him away from his wife. I had to take really good care of Callum now.

'Is he going to be OK?' I asked.

They shrugged as if to say, 'Hey, we're guides, not doctors.'

Finally, the young porter said, 'Sure, it will be OK,' but I could tell he wasn't convinced.

'What about the storm? That was a mistake, right? There is no storm?'

Another shrug. 'We wait and see.'

They built the tent around us as we lay on the sleeping bags. I heard their soles crunch on the stones outside. Then the tent was up and, although it was still light outside, it was dark inside and I realised I was warmer than I had been for hours and actually I was quite glad we had stopped. They told me to zip up tight. I wasn't to leave the tent. I guess I didn't really listen to them otherwise I would have been more scared.

I put my right hand to Callum's dry lips. His lids fluttered close. He smiled. He murmured something and I leaned close, my ear hovering over that sensuous mouth.

'What is it, Callum?'

This time I heard.

'Chelle.' A smile fluttered to his lips, as my smile withered and died.

Oh God, he thought I was her.

'No,' I said lamely, 'I'm not Chelle.' But he carried on, as if I hadn't spoken.

'If I die . . .'

'You're not going to die,' I whispered. 'Honest Cal.' That's what *she* called him. Cal, not Callum. Chelle had tried calling me 'Lor' but had dropped it pretty quick when she saw it didn't cut any ice with me.

'I feel so hot.' He was only wearing a sheet. There was a fire inside me too. 'I'm glad we came. I didn't want to but now you are here, it makes sense. Thank you for looking after me. I know how much you love me.'

'Cal,' I interrupted. I soaked up the sweat on his forehead with a sock.

'Lie next to me.'

I moved under his arm. He didn't smell bad, but he did smell strong. I worked over his chest, stumbling over his rosy nipples. The colour of them was the healthiest thing about him. I moved my hand over his flat belly. It wasn't hard but not soft either. He couldn't afford to lose any more weight.

He needs a good wash, I told myself unconvincingly. He needs to be cleaned. I trailed the makeshift flannel over his damp skin and down, down, to the line of sweet hair. I toyed with the tiny buttons of his boxer shorts and then lowered them. Before my eyes his penis unravelled and staked me out; a one-eyed worm up to look at the world. My old friend. My *big* old friend. I could just touch him there. Just to see what would happen. Just to see how ill he was.

'Mmm,' he kept saying. I knew what *that* meant. 'Don't stop,' he murmured approvingly.

'Oh, Callum,' I sighed before correcting myself quickly. 'I mean, Cal.'

I kissed his dry lips. I couldn't resist. No one would know. He would never know.

But *I* knew. I stopped. Christ! Talk about kicking a man when he's down! I sat there, looking at his dick and I thought, would he really want this? If he were in his right mind would he really want me to ... to play with his prick?

'Chelle, what are you doing?'

Oh shit.

'Nothing, nothing at all!'

'Oh, don't stop, baby,' he said. 'Touch me more ...'

What was I doing? His penis was like a stick of rock and I was stealing candy from a baby. I'll say one thing for Chelle, she knew a good cock when she found one. I put my lips against it. I breathed on it, like you blow hot soup, and I moved my tongue, and then I shifted so that I was in a prime spot. I pulled his cock. I held back the foreskin and devoted myself to the beautiful head. I explored the tender folds of skin, the pulsing veins, that hard velvet softness.

I wanted him to come inside my mouth. I adored that cock. There was nothing half-hearted about this. This would be the best blow-job in the whole world: two hands, one very busy tongue and lips that could suck blood from a stone. It wasn't safer to go slower. Much better to go fast, before he could stop me. I wanted to give him so much pleasure that he would have to get better soon. I wanted to give him so much pleasure that he would think it was a dream. And while he was coming in my mouth he wouldn't, couldn't, be coming in hers. When he was coming in my mouth he was mine, all mine. As he juddered, a thousand ancient judders, he whispered, 'Thank you, thank you,' and then he pulled my hair. 'Chelle, thank you.'

I thought I had made him better.

That evening, Callum wouldn't eat again and I sat by his sleeping bag, afraid that the guides were right, that we were doing too much. Maybe the descent was too fast. Could he get some kind of bends like this?

At about ten o'clock I went out to speak to the porters. There was this strange mist heading towards me. I couldn't make out my hand. Even my feet were lost. It sounds strange but at first I didn't realise what it was; it was snow. Someone grabbed me. It was the young porter. He shouted. He shouted lots of times before I could make out the words: 'Get back in the tent.'

I gripped him closely. I could feel his breath on my cheek. His cheek was white. The snow was settling on him. My nose was already covered. My hands were freezing. I couldn't move my fingers.

'What's happening?' I asked. Later, I would think, what an idiot I am! Why did I need to ask? Wasn't it obvious? But at the time I needed to *hear* it. I needed to be told it before I could accept it.

'Big storm. Look after him.'

'I can't. He's sick. I need help.'

'Nothing to do,' he said. He pushed me back into the

tent. I almost tripped on Callum lying there in his bag. 'We wait.'

You've seen those toys that people bring back from holiday? Those little glass domes containing little statues of the Eiffel Tower, Big Ben or wherever and you shake them and they get covered with a beautiful sprinkling of fine white snow. This wasn't like that at all. The snow that fell here was wet and cold and once it arrived it didn't budge. We were on one of the most exposed slopes of the Anapurna circuit. We were in the hands of cowboys and fools. The wind and the snow battered at the tent like a monster trying to get in. I worried we would be blown away. I didn't know which scared me more, dying in a fall or surviving it. We wait, the young porter had said. That's all we could do. I just held on to Callum. My tears fell on to his sleeping bag. I don't think he realised a thing.

After Dave told me about Rose Connelly, I watched her. I watched the way she walked into the pub ignoring everyone until someone said 'hello', and then she went, 'Oh! Hi!' like she was really surprised to see them there. I watched the way she fiddled with her shirt buttons when she spoke to men – even the drunk men who would chat up anyone. She was on that cusp between beautiful and ugly. Her teeth were all wrong but there was something endearing and sexy about them. She had this perma-tan and wild hair too; I think it was naturally curly but she had a perm on top of that, as was the fashion, and it went haywire. I don't think her body was so great. She was pear-shaped but she dressed to cover it up. And she was promiscuous. She had been to the Catholic school and, like most of the girls who had, she had something to prove. There were many rumours about her. Some girls attracted more rumours than others and, with her, they stuck. Apparently she had fucked Dave on the end of the pier while a crowd cheered her on. Apparently she had had four guys in one night on the pool table above O'Harts. 'She was like a machine,' they said. 'Got on the table and asked for it. She got them to form an orderly queue with their hard-ons at the ready.' Maybe it was because of the way she looked – her teeth, I mean – but everyone said that she was the queen of sucking off. They said she gave two boys blow-jobs at the same time. Literally, I mean – had their cocks in her mouth at once. She didn't like receiving oral sex apparently. She said it was dirty and gave you thrush. These things I knew. And now I knew something else about her. This thing I didn't want to know.

When I woke, the tent was in blackness. Chelle was right; it was tight and cosy. For a moment I forgot the danger and just listened to the sound of Callum's breathing. What is better than to wake up next to the man you love? Perhaps not to be suspended up in a mountain in a storm would have been better.

The dark at that moment was unlike any I had ever experienced before. The snow was piled high on top of the tent and either side of us too. You could feel the heaviness of the canvas. Were we going to be buried alive? No one would ever find us. We would freeze to death. It would be slow.

Don't think about that. Think of something funny. I had always fancied doing it on a helicopter with a sniffer dog. Only joking! No, with a pilot who might be called Ralph.

Ralph and I would wear boiler suits and every time we want to have sex we would have to go through a series of zips. Mind your pubes, Ralph.

Callum was waking up. His hand, tightening around

my waist, sent erotic messages all the way down me. I couldn't help feeling horny when he touched me, yet it shocked me. It appalled me a little. In this situation, even when we might die, did I still have to think of sex? I couldn't see Callum but I managed to fumble towards his shape.

'What's happening?' he mumbled.

'It's OK,' I muttered. 'Don't worry!'

I pulled his arm. I wanted to see his watch. It showed four o'clock. I thought it was afternoon but I couldn't be sure. Day and night were merging together.

When I had taken his wrist, Callum must have thought I was feeling for him for he pulled me tightly to him as if he too wouldn't have wanted to be any-where else in the world.

'Well, good morning to you!'

So maybe it wasn't day, after all.

Our lips found each other in the shadows. We kissed. Why did it feel like they had never been away? I stroked his forehead. In the blackness, we needed to feel for each other even more to compensate for our blindness. Our hands became our eyes. I felt for his fingers and he touched my hand, then trailed towards the top of my legs. Was it because of the darkness that my skin was so much more sensitive than usual? Every touch made me want to cry out.

We might die, I told myself. We really might die here! But the only feeling that produced was that we had nothing to lose. We had nothing to fear. OK, we might die. So what? This time I didn't feel so guilty. Callum might not have been 100 per cent but he was at least conscious.

His fingers told him I was ready. I was soaking. I reached for his cock. Yes, it was hard. It didn't take much rubbing up and down to make it rigid. I loved the way it responded to my long strokes. How could it be so hard? I felt my way around the shaft. I teased his balls. His fingers were inside me. His fingers were back home. He should never have been away. I was wet and warm; he was so welcome there. And everything of him I touched felt so alive. I couldn't stop sighing, even though I was scared because Chelle might not groan and sigh as loud as this, yet, however excited I was, I knew exactly what I was doing. I didn't want Callum to come out of the illusion that he was with Chelle, but ... oh, mmm. It was mmm.

And then he begged me to get on top of him and, even though it was too soon, a little unseemly maybe, I steered his prick to my wetness. I gripped his cock tight – how could it be so stiff? – and pushed him in the way I liked it. I sat back on him, so I was right on top of him and I took care of him like a proper nurse. I was healing him, working my medicine. I knew this would either kill him or bring him back to life.

'Chelle?' he said once he was inside me.

'Yes?' I said, although that wasn't, strictly speaking the right answer to that question.

'Oh, baby!'

'Oh, yes!'

There was nothing else I could say. Callum was inside me! My darling was back. His cock filled me up. His fingers pinched my tits. There was just him and me in the silent blackness, his cock was moving up and down me. I ground into him, and he gripped my sides ferociously so that he went deeper, deeper each time. He was filling me up like I hadn't been fucked for a long time. He was making the pace, making a rhythm. I couldn't stop now. Not now. I rode down on him, firm in the saddle, howling.

There were noises outside, only everything was

indistinct and muffled like I was wearing earphones. And when I shimmied out of the sleeping bag, it was freezing; it wasn't like any cold I had encountered before. It wasn't like a cold spell in England, it wasn't damp or fuzzy or even cloudy, and it was as though the air were full of ice. It was like this ice was pointing, digging into our cheeks, like daggers.

'What's happening?' I called out.

'Stay in tent.'

The other porter's voice came, 'Much danger.'

I looked at Callum sleeping. I thought, much danger in here too.

A few minutes later, the flap of the tent was unzipped. The young porter's face was completely covered in snow. I managed not to exclaim too loudly even though I had really wanted to scream.

'We go to check on the others.'

'You think they're in trouble?' It hadn't occurred to me that the others, who were probably much higher than us, might have been worse affected.

Now I thought about it, I was more than petrified. And they only had Raj too. Raj, who was no good to anyone.

'We go see.'

Cal would never get over it if Chelle got hurt. And what about Stella, sweet Stella? She didn't deserve this.

'I'll come too.' I pulled my jumper and my coat to me.

'No, you stay here, look after him.'

I couldn't leave Callum. I knew that really. They had said it too. I had to look after him.

A few minutes later, I had another question. 'When will you be back?' But they had already gone. Even their footprints had disappeared.

The snow continued to fall. The canvas ceiling of our

tent began, very slowly, to sag. There was nothing to do except to make sure the hours passed as best as they could. And I had to make sure that he didn't know it was me with him and not the love of his life; I think he might have dropped dead if he realised.

I don't think I slept. I watched Callum mostly and I cried a little. I thought of my family and my friends in England. They wouldn't believe this at first, but then slowly they might say, 'Yes, but you know, Lauren always loved the mountains, and she was with Callum? Her first love! How marvellous. What a way to go.'

But I didn't want to go.

I tried to leave the tent but we were completely snowed in. We would have to be dug free. I called out but no one replied. We were completely alone. The porters had gone. They might be dead by now.

When Callum woke he was a little hungry. I supposed that was a good sign, in the short term at least. I fed him rice mixed with a little water. I couldn't see him at all in the darkness, so I kept missing his mouth. This made him laugh, so I let it make me laugh even though I didn't think anything was funny any more. We didn't have much water either. The porters had kept the other bottles in their tent.

Then I had to help Callum to pee into a bottle. I didn't mind. I held his penis, wishing I could see it. Even when flaccid, even when curled up against his thigh, that cock felt lovely. I wanted to make it stiff. I wanted to feel the transformation. I loved the way it went from sleeping to awake. I loved that hard-on.

But it was so cold.

'Lie next to me,' he said. When I was in place, he held me tight.

'Is it bad?' Callum asked. 'Tell me.'

Our porters had disappeared. He was sick and needed

to get lower or else. We were stuck in rising snow. We were close to running out of food and water. Bad was one way of putting it.

I chose another way.

'It's all under control,' I said.

'So do you think we're going to make it?'

'Yes, of course.'

But Callum tugged my hand. He couldn't see my face because of the darkness, but he ran his fingers over my lips.

'Why don't you tell me the truth?'

'I don't know but, do you blame me?'

The silence was incredible. It was broken only by the thuds of snow hitting the ground outside.

'If these are my last moments,' Callum whispered, 'then I'm glad I'm with you.'

'With me?'

Who, I was thinking, who exactly do you mean?

'You, baby.'

I didn't like this conversation. 'Is there anything you ... you want to do?'

'Just being here with you, babe, that's enough.'

I remember as a kid saying I wasn't scared of death. Not just as a kid, I said it in my twenties too. 'I'm not afraid to die!' I proclaimed, like I was the only one. I know why I said it. It was because death seemed so remote; it didn't even seem a possibility. Now that it was an inevitability, now it was within reach, now I was afraid, I *didn't* want to die.

The afternoon Dave told me that Callum and Rose would be together, I was in a terrible state. I stayed at home in the morning and tried on some of the presents Callum had bought me: the blue silk nightdress, the red basque and the cream French knickers. I looked at myself in the mirror for hours. I don't know what I wanted to see. I felt terrible. I knew something bad was on its way, yet at the same time I felt unbearably horny. I don't think I had ever felt as desperate for sex as I did then. And I think it was the first time that I wanted sex. I mean, usually I wanted Callum; this was the first time I thought that Callum would be nice but sex would be better.

I wanted to be fucked.

Callum had given me some perfume the same week. It came in a beautiful bottle, the outline of a woman; it was a bit like a Klimt picture, all curves and golden. I found myself rubbing it up and down my thighs. I was so hot. I was swinging backwards and forwards, willing myself. I pushed the bottle up. I arched my back and thought of him and how much I loved him and how much, when we had sex, I wanted him to ram me harder and my face contorted but I didn't care, because he said he loved it when I really went for it.

According to Dave, they would be around K's, the most expensive clothes shop in town, at about five o'clock. I was there. I waited outside from 4.30, just in case. I was still red from my adventures with the perfume bottle.

It was a wet afternoon, the kind of day that is no good to anyone. Callum hated the rain and I hated the rain. We had that in common, I told myself. We had more than that in common. We loved each other, didn't we? We fucked each other nearly every night. We said we loved each other every time we fucked.

For a moment, those bonds between us seemed very frail indeed.

What would happen when we ran out of water? I cursed myself for allowing the porters to go. Chelle would have insisted they stayed. It was my fault.

'I can feel your fear,' Callum said.

'I'm not scared,' I lied.

'Don't be,' he said. 'Make love to me. If we're really going to die then that's the way I want to go.'

Was it my imagination or was it getting slightly brighter in the tent? I thought Callum knew who I was. He must have known. How could he not? But then he said, 'Come on, Chelle. Come here. Sit on me,' and I didn't know what to think. His hands were weak but his suggestions weren't. Outside, snow fell to the ground. I wondered if it was starting to thaw. I edged slowly up his body, careful not to squash him.

'Are you sure?'

'Come on,' he said, and he was quite impatient. 'Sit on my mouth, please.'

'Well I . . . since you ask so politely.'

I don't know where he got the strength from. He hauled me over him. I didn't know what to do at first. What if he realised who I was? Then I had an idea.

'Callum, I'm going to turn myself around.'

This way I had his cock in my mouth and my cunt was in his face. It was gloriously obscene. I was on the roof of the world. I couldn't concentrate, never can, so I decided to let this be my time, or rather Chelle's time, for that's whose pussy he was eating so hungrily, whose clit he was licking so generously.

'Oh, yes!' he kept breathing into my pubes. 'Fucking hell, oh yes, bounce down on me baby, harder.'

'Callum, Cal, I mean, you're not well enough,' I whispered to his cock.

'You're making me better. I'm going to rub your medicine all over my face. I want more of it. I want more of your stuff. It makes me better.'

His hands gripped my waist and pulled me up and down on him. I was speechless now, thank goodness, or

I'm sure I would have given myself away. Christ, if this is what he could do when he was sick, think what he could do when he was better!

I didn't think I would sleep but I must have dropped off because I woke to the sound of him calling me, or rather, calling her.

'What is it? Cal, I'm here.'

'Come closer to me.'

He tried to kiss me, but I was growing scared now. He was almost himself; it wouldn't take long before he came out of this state and realised he wasn't dreaming. I turned my head from him.

'Go back to sleep,' I said. I had to be cruel to be kind.

'I won't sleep,' he said plaintively. 'We'll sleep when we're dead. I need my medicine.'

'What medicine? Don't be silly, Cal.'

'You know what I mean.'

Callum wriggled down the sleeping bag and started pulling at my jeans. He yanked down the zip and then he tugged at my knickers. His fingers weren't as cold as they had been. He lowered himself down my body and put his mouth against my pelvis and breathed.

'You've still got plenty of medicine for me, haven't you?'

'Shh,' I said. He pulled my jeans down my butt.

'You drive me crazy. You smell so good. I can smell all your beautiful juices. I can recognise you from miles away. I just have to sniff and I know its you.'

I tried to push him away but he was nibbling away at my panties like they were the icing on his birthday cake. And then he pulled them to one side, revealing my pubic hair and he just kind of blew there. I lay back, helpless. The jeans kind of locked me into position.

'Fucking hell, you're soaking.'

Then he ducked his head down. I was swept away on this wave of gorgeousness. He was licking me there. And then he did something else, it was like he was sucking me and I didn't know how he did it. No one had ever done that to me before.

'What are you doing?'

He raised his head and I gripped hold of it. Down boy, we haven't finished yet. It was great. I had been licked before, but never sucked. I was fearless. No one knew. No one could say I was doing anything wrong. We might die! I pulled off my jeans. I rolled over so my arse was pressed against his groin. Fuck, was he hard!

'I want it this way.'

'From behind?'

'Sure, why not?' I said. He was massaging my cheeks and it felt amazing. A bit cold but amazing.

'You don't normally.'

'Don't I?'

'No.'

'It must be the mountain air. Or the honeymoon, or ...'

'I'm not complaining, I'm just saying, it's a bit odd, that's all.'

'Well ...'

'You usually hate it like that. You say it makes you feel like an animal.'

Oh fuck. How long could I do this for? He was going to find out. He was definitely going to find out.

'I feel like an animal now.'

'Do you, babe?'

'Yes. We are on honeymoon, aren't we? It's time we experimented a little.'

At first, I just lay down with my head in the pillow. I

heard him get prepared behind me. I heard him wank himself harder, and then he fumbled around between my legs.

This wasn't going to work.

I got up on all fours. I stuck out my arse. He just kneeled there and waited. I wriggled a little, just to let him know I was ready. And then his hand was cupping my arse and he was holding me apart down there and then he was fitting himself inside me. Whoosh. I pushed back against him, and his sharp intake of breath told me exactly how much he was enjoying it. I worked him up and down and then I gripped his hand and put it round my front.

'Rub me,' I told him, 'rub my clit.'

'Like this?'

It was exactly like that.

I saw Rose first. And then I saw Callum. They were running out of the store. I saw their hot flushed faces. I remember the window display of K's was unfinished and the six-foot-tall hairless models with no nipples were naked. I can remember thinking that they shouldn't be left like that. Just because they looked funny, it wasn't fair to humiliate them.

Then I saw Rose's over-bite, the teeth that told you she loved sucking guys off. I knew that he loved being sucked off. I knew what he would say to her as he pushed her down to him. 'Suck me, baby, just like that, baby, oh you know what I like, baby, you're so good to me, baby, don't stop, baby, I'm close to it, baby. I'm close to coming, baby. Can I come in your mouth, baby?'

Their feet hit the wet paving stones. Why are you in such a hurry, Callum? Rose was slower but, ever the gentleman, Callum held back, waiting for her, then when she caught up with him, they both started to walk, very casually, very nonchalant. What would you call them if you saw them like that? I saw the look that passed between them. Jubilant? Exultant? I think the only way I can explain it was that they looked like they couldn't believe their fucking luck.

'Let's do it again.' He tried to kiss me, but I pushed him off. It was pitch black in the tent but, even so, Callum was gaining power by the hour. He would soon be able to tell who I really was. His temperature had come right down too.

But he played and tickled me and tweaked at my breasts and nudged me with his hard-on and swirled his tongue in my mouth and it was very, very difficult, perhaps even pointless, to resist. He worked my cunt with his fingers. I could feel the juices flow.

'Let's do it the other way around again,' I proposed.

I couldn't see him but I knew he was smiling.

'Only if I can put it up your arse!' he said.

Christ! 'I thought you weren't well.'

'I'm feeling a lot better.'

'You want to ... fuck me up the arse?'

'Yeah, I want to fuck your tight little arsehole.' His fingers were so good too. It was very hard to think straight.

'I don't normally let you, do I, Cal?' I kept my voice as neutral as possible.

'You've never let me but, honey, we might die. Do you really want to die denying me that? I thought, after today, you might want to. C'mon baby, it will feel so tight and deep, and I'll be very gentle.'

'I ...'

'Oh, darling, you've looked after me so well, I just want to look after you.'

In what way was that looking after me? I wondered.

And then I thought, if I had to let him go, wouldn't it be funny to send Callum back to her, demanding it all the time?

I put a pillow under my pelvic bone and lay down with my back slightly arched so that I had a nice round of arse for him to go with. He was behind me, my love. He parted my buttock cheeks very gently and very carefully. I felt the space fill with air. I could feel he was in control and I let him be in control and I tried to relax but I didn't really have to, because actually I wanted it. I really wanted to feel his cock up me.

I didn't mind where exactly.

'Are you sure you want to go through with this?'

'Uh huh.' He was pushing around my hole, not quite there yet, but he didn't let up the pressure in my pussy – not for one moment. I was nearly coming from that alone, so the thought of more, more cock up me, was fantastic. He lubricated his finger and I felt him swish around inside me. It felt rude and disgusting. It felt fucking amazing.

We didn't do *this* sixteen years ago.

Then, when he thought I was ready for it, he took his finger out and I was about to groan my displeasure, please don't stop, when I could feel his dick pressing against my arse, ready to take its turn.

'Are you sure?'

I wished he wouldn't keep asking me. How many times do you have to say yes before they believe you?

'Oh, yes.'

'Yes?' he asked. 'Sure?'

'*Yes*,' I shouted through gritted teeth. 'Fuck me, there, now.'

He was very slow and he was very thorough. I could feel his cock move up me, take over my arse, and it made me burn but at the same time it made me very, very excited. At first I couldn't move. I just had to be as still as a statue, adjusting to the size of him, but then, as the pressure on my clit grew and as I grew accustomed to that wonderful swelling or throbbing, I felt my pelvis rock, just gently, just quietly, backwards and forwards.

'You naughty girl,' he hissed in my ear. 'You fucking love it, don't you? You love being screwed up the arsehole.'

And I wanted to say no, I wanted to say I didn't, that, actually, I preferred it the normal way, but I couldn't help myself and I was pushing harder and harder and he was really fucking me now. I mean, he was slamming in and out and in and out. This was as dirty as it gets. He was pushing as hard as he could. He didn't care that he might tear me but neither did I. We both had the same goal of fucking glorious pleasure and that was enough.

It felt as if I had been impaled on a stick, but what a stick it was.

'Oh, Christ,' he cried. 'How am I ever ...'

I never found out what he was going to say and he never told me. I didn't know what he meant. When he lay down I wiped his forehead and asked him about it. But he fell into a deep sleep. From the look on his face, he seemed quite content.

The next morning, the snow slid off the canvas sides of the tent and I could hear digging. The porters were back. I let Callum sleep and opened the flaps of the tent.

'Did you see them? Are they OK?' I hugged the porter and he looked surprised.

'Were you worried?'

'I was fucking petrified!' I admitted.

He smiled. 'And him, you looked after him?'

'Yes!' I blushed.

'The others keep going.' He pointed up to the sky.

'Up?' I couldn't believe it. They were still pressing on with their foolhardy adventure. Poor Stella. Chelle had her wrapped round her finger. In more ways than one, obviously.

'Up!'

'It's not too dangerous?'

He shrugged.

He and the other porter debated whether to make Callum a stretcher or not. They decided they would. He slept as they knotted clothes and sleeping bags around him as we dismantled the camp. As they carried him over the stones and the stretcher bobbed around like a little lost ship, he continued to sleep.

We walked for hours. Callum slept. And then the porters, who were ahead, shouted at me. 'Hurry, hurry!' And I dropped everything and ran to where they were shouting because I was sure Callum was dead. I had killed him. He had tumbled down the mountain and my life was over.

But it wasn't like that. In front of us the snow had melted, leaving lush grassland, waving rice and fields of green and little roofs of little houses. It was a promised land. It was the most beautiful and the most welcome sight in the world.

I began to cry.

The young porter put his arm around me. 'It's OK. He better soon,' the young porter said. 'He won't die.'

'You think so?'

'Much better. He gets good medicine.'

'Oh.'

'Very good,' he said, but he turned his back to me so I couldn't see if he was laughing or not. 'No better medicine than that.'

* * *

Two days later, we reached a small bungalow that was the medical centre. The doctor saw Callum straight away. I didn't understand all that he said but I understood that Callum was near death: hallucinations, shivering, the lot. Callum looked about him dreamily. Even in this strange world, he was in a world of his own. I felt quite proud of his list of symptoms. The nurse said that he was very handsome. The doctor said he was very lucky. They gave him a lot of drugs; we had reached civilisation. He didn't need my medicine any more.

We got a taxi back to my old hostel, The Everest. I thought, well we did get to Everest after all, and when he got better, I wanted to tell Callum that and I wanted him to laugh. The taxi driver helped me carry him upstairs but I already knew I couldn't stay. Florence Nightingale had better take her lamp somewhere else. The taxi driver kept saying how thin my husband was. The reception staff looked mystified. I had gone away a lesbian but come back married.

'He's not my husband,' I repeated to the guy with the thin caterpillar moustache.

'It's fine,' he said, and then he yelled to the guy next to him, 'Crazy English girls, eh?'

I couldn't stay in the room. Instead I went to the market. I bought watermelons and strawberries. I searched for foods that would make him stronger but didn't require cooking or preparation. I came back with bags of breads. I wondered what it would be like to shop for him every day. To always make sure that he had dinner on the table. To always make sure he was eating well. Once, the thought of doing that for someone, a man, would have made me laugh.

As I was unpacking the stuff and arranging it on the bedside table, Callum woke.

'It's you! Christ! What ... what day is this?'

He looked stricken. Perhaps he thought it was still the 1980s. Perhaps I could pretend that Haircut One Hundred were still top of the charts and I had on a ra-ra skirt.

'It's OK. You were ... you are on honeymoon with Chelle. You were in the mountains. I just brought you here, that's all.'

And we'll all go down to meet her when she comes.

'So where is she?'

He looked around him in such astonishment. I couldn't blame him for that. Where was she? For once, the implication of her leaving him really hit home.

'She thought it was safer –' I said uneasily (It's always the messenger who gets shot) '– if I brought you down.'

'Safer?' he repeated incredulously. He did have a point!

'Yes. She'll be here soon anyway. All you have to do is wait.'

'OK,' he said feebly.

All I had to do was go. I didn't belong here any more. My work was done. Callum didn't seem to know what was happening to him. He kept saying, 'But ... but why?' and trying to raise himself off the pillow. It reminded me of the last time I saw him, sixteen years ago, in my bedroom with the TV on and the way he seemed about three steps behind.

'I have to go. I can't stay any longer. You'll be all right now.'

When I turned around, he had managed to pull himself out of bed. His feet were on the floor but he was hunched over like he was going to be really sick.

12

The taxi driver laughed as small children waved at us. The journey was taking much longer than I thought it would. Not only did the car struggle at 30 kph but we had to stop and wait for ages. There were too many buffalo in the way. The taxi driver said we had to hurry because the monastery would be impossible to find in the dark. I didn't know how worried he was because he laughed as he explained, but I was worried. I didn't fancy spending the night in a windowless car. The temperature was plummeting as we moved away from the city and up the mountain roads. I was hungry too though, and so he stopped at a café. There was a choice of chicken curry or pizza. I chose the curry. There was a discussion. The waitress, the cook and the owner all joined in. Apparently, chicken would take up to three hours; not only would they have to wring the chicken's neck, but they would have to find a chicken first. I said a pizza would do fine, thank you.

After I checked out The Everest I went straight to the taxi rank. I knew I had to get myself together and where better to do that than a monastery? There, the only thing I would have to worry about was whether I had cleared my mind from worry enough.

Now was *my* time, I decided.

As we drove the sky grew blacker. Night fell earlier in the mountains. The taxi driver was confused and apologetic. I was worried now, not so much for me any more, but him too.

He seemed to be driving completely blind. It was like swimming underwater with your eyes shut.

'Here maybe, a slip road, miles down,' then he said, disappointed, 'Arggh, it's not here.'

'Are we lost?'

He let out a roar of relief. 'I see a light there.'

The light was a very long way away, and according to the map, it wasn't where it should have been, but we headed towards it anyway. We parked and then got out of the car. The taxi driver insisted on walking me to the gates.

'This is a very good monastery,' he said. 'It's very famous. People go there when they are –' he mimed a distressed face '– then they come back –' this time he showed me a calm face. 'Very good, yes?'

'Yes. I've heard a lot about it,' I said. All I could think of was Callum's feet hovering over the floor as he pulled himself up. 'Safer? Why safer? Where is Chelle?'

A small man in a saffron robe met us. He had a kindly face. I was glad. He looked like a monk should look; he didn't have any of your new-fangled right-on monk stuff. This was the real Monk McCoy. He chatted with the driver and the driver said that he would come back on Friday.

'You only stay one week,' the little man said. I couldn't tell if it was a question or statement.

'Yes, is that ... is that a problem?'

'It is best you start tonight then.'

'Whatever.'

'Cleanse first. OK?'

In the shower room I had a faint sensation that I was being watched but I peeped out the wooden slats and could see nothing. After the wash I went to my room. It was there that I first felt this wave of pain. I had nearly died up there, for fuck's sake, and now I felt what I can only describe as a wave of incredible homesickness, but it was certainly not for my parents or the house that I had left fourteen years ago. I supposed it was for Callum. He was my home. He was where I wanted to be. I missed him so much. It was physical. It was an earthquake in my stomach. Nothing would ever be good again.

There was a knock on the door. I knew it couldn't be Callum but I wasn't thinking straight just then and, for a moment, I thought I might have conjured him up. I would have given anything for it to have been him. I regretted leaving him alone in The Everest but I knew that although he didn't want me to go then, he would have wanted me to go as soon as he remembered.

Of course it wasn't Callum. It was the small man in the saffron robe. He peered in and smiled.

'Was the shower pleasing for you?'

'Yes,' I said. 'Very clean. I am very . . .' I paused, trying to find a word ' . . . cleansed.'

'Cleansied?' the monk said, rhyming it with frenzied. 'You will be.'

Just as he was about to go, he appeared to have second thoughts; he turned back to me.

'You feel pain now. It is a great loneliness, but it will go.'

'I'm fine,' I lied. How dare he try to analyse me?

'You *will* be fine,' he said, as though he were correcting me. When he smiled his eyes almost disappeared.

My first couple of days at the monastery were hard work. I'm not going to bullshit now. It was hard physical labour and, by day three, I was wiped out. I might have felt better if I hadn't been kept away from everyone. The monks were segregated from guests, but I rarely saw either. In fact, I hardly saw anyone. Meals were eaten in my room. Tasks were done on my own. This was isolation but far from splendid. I don't think it made me calm as the taxi driver suggested. It made me panicky. What made it lonelier was that I couldn't help feeling like something was going on elsewhere, like everyone else was having a good time without me. I never saw anything but sometimes I would hear noises, chuckles or laughs from other rooms, but when I went to investigate, there was nothing. I thought days, weeks had passed, but in fact I had only been there two nights. I began to lose track of time.

I wondered what Callum was doing. Would they look after him in The Everest? Would they make sure he was fed and clean? What if he needed me? I imagined they called in a nurse. I was so replaceable it was painful. They would call in a real nurse; perhaps Callum would be cheeky with her. Perhaps she would wear fishnet stockings under her uniform. She would flash her bottom at him when she leaned over to give him her medicine. Perhaps she would fall for him. He would probably leave Chelle for her. You hear of that, don't you? Stories of men who leave their wives, not for their mistress but for someone they hardly know.

Callum, please don't go.

I imagined Stella and Chelle probably snuggled up together every night. I bet they were licking and stroking, all fingers and fucking. I wouldn't let myself think of Chelle's legs and her orange trainers. I thought of the tea houses and all the sense of freedom I had experienced up there and that feeling of being close to nature. And now, nature had deserted me.

The night I saw Callum with Rose Connelly we fucked in my bedroom, on my bed, between fresh sheets and under my red, orange and cream duvet. My mother was religious about doing the washing and, although I used to complain about it, since my sex life had taken off I had begun to see the benefits. What better to fall back on, to fuck madly on, than freshly laundered smoothness?

There were still sometimes stains on my sheets though and, although I knew they weren't, I used to say they were his come. He said they were me, and that could have been true. I was always wet when I was with him, gushing with it. Sometimes, when he held me apart, just to have a look and a touch with his soft, meaty fingers, I would feel myself almost ejaculate, spurt out this creamy juice, and when he came up to see me, his face would be glistening. The film of my pleasure would mirror his own.

Sometimes we pulled my bedroom curtains, sometimes we didn't. That time, I remember, we did. I made the room dark and turned myself into a shadow, a dark outline. I could have been anyone.

I pushed him down, straddled him. He said, 'Stop, wait a moment, baby. I've got a present for you. It's in my bag.'

Still sitting on his hard-on, I reached down and pulled his bag close. Callum never had the presents in a matching bag. That day's bag was from a supermarket – I knew it didn't reflect the contents. Somehow, I intuitively knew this present would be quite a memorable one.

'Why did you get me a present?' I asked tersely.

'Because...'

'What is it?'

'It's for you,' he said, avoiding the question. 'Something you'll like, I'm sure.'

It was a necklace. I knew it was expensive. And I knew what this was. I read enough of the agony aunt pages to recognise a guilt present when I was given one. He was the man who got me everything. I only had to say my shoes were tired and new ones would come to me. I knew what it was now though. They were what made it all right for him to get sucked by Rose Over-bite Connelly. If he got something for me then he could go to her guilt-free. Taking care of both of us, he was.

I still didn't tell him what I knew though.

First things first.

I rode him. I rode him with our clothes on. Both of us were in jeans, and the feel of the denim, his and mine, was gorgeous. And then we slid our zips down, he did me, and I did him, and all the while I was thinking, this is the last time, and you don't know it. And I was determined to give him a good time, the best time, so that I would be anchored in his heart, so that no one else could compare themselves to me. This had been my life, my existence, for ten months, and now he, he was taking it away, not me.

I let him come in my mouth one last time. I had noticed he tasted different sometimes, depending on what he had eaten. That night he was thick and creamy. It was fast and memorable in my throat.

That's your last time, baby. I pushed him away.

'Get out,' I said, and I was as cold as I could be. To show just how much I didn't care, I switched on the TV. It was 'Play Your Cards Right'. Bruce Forsyth rubbed his chin and laughed at the contestants who didn't seem to know where they were or what was expected of them.

'What?' Callum's mouth twitched. Was I joking? I *had* to be joking. And for one moment, I was tempted. 'Oh yes, only kidding.' But then I thought of the two of them running out the shop with their red shiny cheeks. They didn't exactly belong in a best gags book. And the way he waited for her.

'Get out?'

'Higher. Higher. Lower.'

The studio audience screamed their disapproval. Callum was standing completely still. How silly he looked naked. His dick was hanging down, redder than the rest of him; the curve of his balls was really quite comical. I had to tell myself this, otherwise I would have got up and hugged him.

Callum got dressed wordlessly. One day I would learn that Callum was unusual among men because he put on his T-shirt first, before he put on his boxers, that is. At the time, I didn't know it was remarkable. I didn't know anything was remarkable. I had nothing to compare.

'I know about you and Rose.'

'Rose?' he said, but he didn't seem surprised; it was more like he thought this conversation was inevitable. He pulled on his shorts and knelt at my feet. His face said sorry.

'Yup. I know what you've been getting up to, and I hate it. You disgust me.'

'I . . . we shouldn't have. I'm so sorry.'

The fact that he didn't deny it was the biggest shock of all. I guess I had been prepared for him to talk me round, to lie, and maybe, yes, against the evidence, I would have accepted his lie. I would have said, 'Oh, I'm just being silly. It was just something I heard,' and he would have come up with three or four good reasons why he and Rose weren't doing it, and why the fact that they ran out of a shop together wasn't evidence of guilt. But he didn't do any of that. This shamefaced apology was the one thing I hadn't anticipated and it was the worst thing of all.

Day three I was told to do some weeding. The garden was deep, light, beautiful. The lawn shone emerald green, like a pool. Each side was decorated by beds of flowers. At the other end of the garden I saw some monks wandering around chanting. I hoped they might come over.

I got into my work. My knees dug into the ground. This is satisfying, I told myself. This is the life. I am here. I am learning about myself. For the first time, I was glad that there was space between Callum and me. I heard a rustling sound behind me. A monk was standing there, looking at me. He was closer to me than anyone else had been over the last few days.

'Hello,' I said. I was eager for conversation but the monk didn't say anything. He gestured for me to continue. I scowled at him, disappointed, and got back to my work. But he didn't go.

'You've been here three days,' he said, after a long pause in which he could surely have thought up something more interesting than that. It seemed I had Monk Einstein here.

'Yup, that's right,' I said. I turned to face him. I can't talk to someone without looking them in the eye, but again he gestured at me to continue weeding. To tell the truth, it kind of annoyed me. Who did he think he was? My dad?

Still, I pulled out the weeds and threw them on the pile. The sun had warmed my shoulders and I was sweating slightly. I pushed the hair out of my eyes. I realised that I smelled a little. I was going to move on to the next patch when the monk finally spoke again.

'Feeling whoopee?'

'I'm sorry?' I thought I had misheard. I thought he had said whoopee. He repeated the question and I realised that he had.

It must have been some reference to the whole process.

'Erm, I feel like it's working. The whole regime is doing me some good, I think. It's clearing my mind.'

'Ahhh,' he said. 'Feeling whoopee?'

This time, the monk didn't have to gesture for me to go back to work. I had been desperate to talk to someone, yet I had landed myself with the monastery's resident idiot. I got on with the weeds. But the next one I tried wouldn't come out. As much as I pulled, it was embedded in the earth. It was a stubborn one.

The monk leaned down and whipped it out from the ground.

I smiled my thanks before I realised his hand was now on my leg.

'Ummm, hello?' I said and pointed at his hand. 'My thighs aren't weeds. I'm flattered you think that but . . .'

'Carry on,' he said sharply. So I did and, as I yanked at the roots, his hand carried on there until there was definitely no mistake; the guy was circling my legs in a predatory kind of way.

And I was letting him.

Perhaps I didn't explain something. Monk Einstein was hot. You've seen the Shaolin monks? There's a guy who does the splits and then bounces down. This Monk was the spit of him, and his hand was working on my thigh. I mean he wasn't Callum, but he was male, right?

I pulled up a weed.

'Feeling good?'

'Um? OK,' I said.

I decided to leave the questions till after. This was no time for philosophy. This was no time for the big what-am-I-doing-here-type enquiries. I had to live for the moment and if anyone deserved it, I did. Callum was a lost fucking cause. A girl has got to eat, hasn't she?

And I was more than a little hungry.

I bent over. And he put his fingers inside me. And

that was the joy of it, I suppose, just weeding as if this was the kind of thing one did every day. Perhaps this explained why gardening was so popular these days.

I started breathing heavily, so that he knew I did quite appreciate his application, and then I just let go. I wasn't encouraging any more; this was all about me. Besides, he didn't need encouraging. His fingers were right up inside me and they were everywhere. He knew what he was doing. I just let him rub me and rub me until it started like a rippling, then the sensations became more and more overwhelming and I was coming, kneeling over his hands, weeding in the monastery garden.

After I had stopped shuddering, I turned around and faced him with this giant green weed in my hand dangling roots.

'What's this all about then?'

'That's a flower,' he said sternly. He straightened up and walked away.

13

'Feeling wicked?'

'Ummm!' Was this a code? 'I'm feeling OK!'

It was the day after the weeding incident and I was elbow-deep in washing up. I had been worrying over the weeding incident for the last twenty-four hours, but there was, of course, no one I could ask about it. Everyone got on with their individual things. This morning I had watched the gardens longingly but Monk Einstein did not appear. Next time, I decided, I wouldn't succumb so easily. I would put up a damn good fight. But nothing had happened.

We had porridge for lunch. It wasn't turning out to be the best of days. Now all the porridge was stubbornly stuck against the side of the pan.

'Feeling scrummy?' the monk said. This monk was not as good-looking as yesterday's. I looked around for some support. None came. There was no one around after all. The not-so-good-looking monk and I were alone. Alone with the pans full of cold leftover porridge.

I whispered, 'I thought we weren't supposed to speak after supper.'

'This is lunch.'

'Oh.' That told me.

So I got back to my work because I can be a conscientious little miss sometimes and there was a lot of gunk stuck to the side of the bowls and I had to get right into it to get it off. I was wearing pink plastic gloves and every time I immersed them in the sink they filled up in warm soapy water.

Something was happening down below. The not-so-good-looking monk was tracing lines on my calves. On second thoughts, he wasn't bad looking. His eyes were puffed up but his expression was very tender, and he had something quite gentlemanly about his nose, if not his behaviour.

'What are you doing?' I asked.

'Feeling fucky?' His fingers tickled the backs of my knees.

'Whoa, whoa, I don't know what you monks are on, but this ... this is not my game ...' I said.

He looked puzzled. 'You had the ritual cleansing four days ago?'

'Ye-es ...'

'OK, so OK ...'

He dived down. This time he raised my gown and stroked the backs of my thighs. He had nice hands, I had to admit. His face was not conventionally handsome but there was nothing wrong with his hands. He had long, slender fingers, fingers that you could take anywhere. They moved to the centre of my thighs. They were working between my legs.

I just carried on washing up. I was determined to play it cool this time. I wasn't going to moan or plead with this one. I scrubbed the white bits off the sides of the wooden bowls. I became breathless but not anxious any more. If this was the way they did things here, then so be it. His hands were going up and up and then I think he kneeled down behind me. Pretty appropriate, I thought, that a monk should kneel, but I never expected one to kneel behind me while I did the washing up. One hand went to my breast. He slid his fingers up my legs, edging his way between my thighs.

'Should I take my knickers off?' I asked.

'This is a monastery,' he said sternly. He squeezed my nipple tight between his fingers.

'OK,' I said, 'I'll take that as a no.'

His fingers felt their way to my panties. They pulled the material aside. I must say, my 'establishment' didn't have a strict door policy at this particular moment in time. I was letting anyone in, but it did feel so good. The monk paused only slightly and then traced my crack from buttocks inwards. He was going in. In, in, in, then his fingers were lightly pressing, prodding at my cunt. How light-fingered he was, stroking and pressing me. I had gone very red. My whole body felt hot. I couldn't stop whimpering a little. And then he was doing what I can only describe as a corkscrew movement. It was like he was drilling into me, whirling around my wet hole.

'Oh yes!'

No. I put down a bowl and picked up another one. This one was also covered in porridge. It may have been mine. I got the wiry brush to scrape it off.

He was using two hands on me now. One hand was cleverly pinching my clit; the other was doing in and out corkscrew fucking motions in my slit. Very clever, I thought. You would never have believed that monks were meant to be celibate. I mean, where the fuck did they learn these things? Did they attend a monk sex school where a lady monk (a monkess?) lay on a bed with her legs spread, holding herself apart so that everyone could have a go. Now that was a job I wouldn't have minded.

The water slopped out of the sink, soaking my front. It probably got him on the head, but he didn't seem to mind. I was struggling with this bowl; it slipped out of my fingers a couple of times.

I couldn't help moving against him just a little bit, but he held me firmly in place. Then he stuck his head up my gown and blew, yes, he just blew warm air, warm breath, into my pussy.

Oh God, he was going to lick me. Here in the kitchens, while I did the washing up.

I reached into the sink and pulled out the saucepan. I knew this would be the hardest job. The porridge had attached itself firmly to the base. The metal was covered with oats.

I felt the wetness of his tongue glide against my crack. Did he taste the slivers of me? Did he feel the shivers of me? His fingers worked at the same time as his tongue. They were a marvellous team, tongue and thumb, lips and fingers, all working to the same goal. He was underneath me.

I got the brush and started to rub really, really hard at the pan. It was good to have something to do with my hands – and something to concentrate on – otherwise I think I would have been lost really. But I was lost anyway. I pushed my buttocks out and rocked ever so slightly so, somehow, I was mounted on top of his head. He was facing upwards to lap me up while I did my work. And then I had to put the pan down and hold the sides of the sink because I was engulfed in this shocking bubbly warmth, and the fingers that were fucking me were getting really fast and hard, and the other fingers that were fondling me were working an incredible rhythm.

Christ, what a tongue!

I sat alone in the meditation room. Every time I thought about it, I lost my breath and had to tell myself to calm down. I had gone for a few minutes without thinking of Callum. That made me feel even guiltier than what I had been doing those few minutes.

I was still so wet between the legs that I thought I might stain the cushions. Then a monk walked in, and I felt a kind of worry and an excitement at the same time. Again? Could I come like that again? Would I *ever* come like that again? The monk sat on a cushion and crossed his legs slowly so that his knees were really high. He was humming. I wanted him to throw his gown aside and fuck me. I would wrap my legs around him and make him thrust into me.

'Feeling whoopee?' I said to him.

He ignored me. In fact, I think he started humming even louder. OK, I decided, it didn't work on everyone.

So that's how the days passed. I would be doing a chore and a monk would come along and he might ask me some bizarre question and no matter what answer I gave – 'Yes, I'm feeling phooey' or 'No, I don't feel fucky' – he would masturbate me until I was throbbing.

I stopped wearing knickers and I walked around in a perpetual state of pre-orgasm. So what if I was alone 99 per cent of the time, that 1 per cent of interaction – interaction? Who was I kidding? Physical contact – was just enough. Who needed conversation? Who needed Callum? I didn't think about him at night. I didn't think about anything. I went to my room and my head hit the pillow and the next thing I knew a bell was ringing for morning meditation and it was 5 a.m. and I was awake with an amazing sense of lightness in my heart and body.

When I weeded, I thought about weeding. When I washed up, I thought about that. And when some monk had his fingers up my fanny, then I thought about that too.

One time, I was in the prayer room lighting incense when a monk who looked exactly like Keanu Reeves came up to me. It was clear that I was expected to just go about my duties while he attended to his duties down below. So I did. I placed the sticks into their wooden holders and lit matches. They smelled magnificent.

Monk Keanu placed his fingers in my pussy and stroked my clit. He shoved his face against my pubic hair and pushed my labia apart so I was exposed. I could feel all of me stretch apart, so I was just a pink hole in his face.

Another time, I was scrubbing the bath when a monk opened the door and came in to watch me. I have to say, I didn't even look up. I didn't even care what my monk of the day looked like any more. A face is a face is a face, right? I do, however, think that monk may have been a Westerner, only because at one point he put his hand over my stomach and I noticed he had hairs on the knuckles. I don't mean to say they were unattractive, they were just there, but that's how I knew. He tilted me over the side of the bath and slid his finger into me. His nails were long but when I told him he was scratching, he rubbed me gently with the pads of his fingers.

'I love being finger-fucked,' I whispered to him, forgetting the silence rule, but his grunt told me that he loved finger-fucking too. I opened as wide as I could to accommodate him even as I carried on scrubbing away at the porcelain sides.

Who would imagine cleaning a bath would be such fun?

And the strangest bit was ... I didn't have to do anything for the monks. I just let them touch me and they seemed quite content with it. Callum? I thought, who gives a damn about you?

* * *

After Callum left my bedroom sixteen years ago, I stayed there for a long time. Over the next few days I only left to use the loo or to make cups of tea. I wanted to be alone. After day four my parents, in their dull lumbering way, demanded that I came downstairs and insisted that I ate dinner with them. They were more worried that I wasn't eating than that my world had crashed. They sat comatose in front of the TV and thought I should do the same. Even when I was there they talked about me as if I weren't. There was talk about spilled milk and there was talk about plenty more fish in the sea.

'She and Callum have had a little tiff,' was the way Mum put it to Dad.

'It's not a little tiff!'

'Teenagers,' offered Dad, as though that explained everything.

I fled upstairs. My pillows smelled of Callum. The next afternoon, Mum tried harder. She made me sit at the table while she cooked beans on toast. I burnt my fingers on the metal spoon in the saucepan.

'Ow!' At last, the tears could come.

'There, there,' Mum said. The inadequacy of her words made everything worse.

'I won't see Callum again.'

'Course you will,' Mum said. I suppose she was right in a way, but I don't think she could have imagined it would be quite like this.

'I mean . . . I won't be his girlfriend any more.'

I could tell from Mum's face that she didn't think that was such a bad thing.

When, a few days later, she washed my pillows I went ballistic and she said, 'I never thought you should be so serious about him anyway.'

I sat in school despising the teachers. Instead of

revising, I looked at the photos of the mountains of the places I had never been to, and probably never would if I stayed with him. I learned about the monasteries where you could learn ways to be happier with yourself.

'Stuff this. I'm going to see the world,' I told everyone. 'I don't care about Callum. I don't care about anyone. I'm going to live my life for me from now on.'

It filled me with a sense of dread.

I was in the garden again when two of them came at me. This was the first time I had had more than one, but I had no objections. One of them fingered my pussy, the second explored my arsehole while I attempted to hang the wet gowns out to dry. I can't tell you how hard it was to keep my equilibrium while my body was being so sensually touched like that. It was a warm day, though, and the gowns were almost dry by the time I managed to peg them up. My fingers were sweaty. The pegs kept slipping through my fingers.

Another time, when I was peeling potatoes, three men came, although the third man was just looking. He was an older monk who I had seen on the first day. I took care not to appear to be neglecting my tasks. I gripped the white potato firmly in my left hand and the peeler in my right. The peeler sliced through the skin which came off into my hand but I could only do small pieces at a time. The sensations down there were too unbearably good, and I had to stop or I would have cut myself.

I woke up about midnight one night, sure that someone was in the room with me. In the shadows I could just make out a monk, one of the potato-peelers. He pressed a finger to his lips and then beckoned me to follow.

'Where are we going?'

Again he shushed me. I padded after him, barefoot. I was wearing the regulation nightdress and nothing else.

After we were out of the building, I asked, 'What's happening?'

This time, he whispered, 'Don't you know it's silent time?'

'And what if I'm not silent?'

'You will be,' he said simply. 'You *must* be.'

I think there were six of them in the dining room including the Shaolin monk and his ugly friend. The other three I hadn't met before, although one of them looked familiar.

Except for a huge oak table in the centre, the room was empty of furniture.

The monk told me to lie on the table. I laughed in his face. Almost immediately, the six stepped forward and frogmarched me over there.

'What the hell is this?'

Up until that moment, their approach had been soft. Now everything was changing.

'This is about desires,' the monk said.

'So it's about your desires now?'

'Not ours,' he said simply and he eased me on to the table. They pulled my legs apart and my arms. I started to resist but realised immediately how futile it was. One against six? Who was I kidding? Besides, I figured, it wasn't like we necessarily were on opposite sides. Then they tied me up. The ties went around my wrists and my ankles. They considered a blindfold. They considered a gag and decided not. For now.

'We want to see if you are cleansed.'

'Is the pope Catholic?' I said. Yes, I still could joke.

They conferred. Finally, one of them tentatively came back, 'Yes?'

Or maybe I couldn't.

I said, 'I mean, it's obvious I'm cleansed. I don't need you to check up on me.'

They ignored me. Then one of the monks stepped forward to explain.

'We are not checking up on you. This is the –' he hesitated, looking for the word '– culmination of your time here. But, so sorry, each time you speak you break the rules.'

'And –' I nodded to my restrained arms and legs '– what if I break the rules?'

'More –' again he was struggling with the appropriate word '– punishment?'

They spun the table around. It was like a particularly bad ride at a funfair. The Waltzer or something. I arrived, with my legs spread, right in front of Monk Keanu.

'Hello,' I said dizzily. The monk and the pussy. I thought that would be a good name for a pub.

Keanu put his finger to his lips. I was just about to say, well this is ridiculous, why do I have to be quiet? when I felt what his other hand was doing. He had put his finger up me. I tensed and then, seconds later, I relaxed. My juice was flowing. He was rubbing me to wetness and, crikey, that was nice. This was going to be fine. Nothing I hadn't done before, at least, except for the gathering of spectators. It was all in a day's work.

It was so nice, in fact, that I thought it was about time I had some more stimulation. Monk Keanu was an expert at this, and his fingers, I don't know how many (three or four maybe?) were making fantastic whirling moves in my cunt and all over my clit. And I was so wet and slippery there, it was embarrassing.

'Please,' I said, fucking thin air, 'fill me up.'

'Shh,' he said.

'Oh, fuck the punishment! Fuck me.'

I don't know if it was because I talked so much that my treatment went on for so long. Daylight came and went. When I needed the bathroom and food they took me and then brought me back. They put me back in the same position with my arms and legs bound, but I think each time they did it so that my arms and legs were spread just a little wider apart, and my pussy was just that little bit more accessible to everyone.

Then the instruments came out. I saw a metal contraption and I groaned.

'There's no way you're putting that up me!' I shouted.

'Shh,' they said.

'Are you experimenting on me?'

Another monk stepped forward.

'Experimenting on pleasure, to meet your desire. But that's all I can say,' he told me.

'You're not putting that thing up my pussy,' I said.

The thing was, they didn't. Even while Keanu was gently tendering my cunt, someone else raised my buttocks and ever so slowly that thing was passed up my arse.

Jesus Christ.

It was terrible at first; I mean, I was no virgin there, but this was cold metal, and it was a funny shape too, I wriggled and I pushed and I thought, Oh God, this is too disgusting.

Keanu watched my grimacing and he worked harder to make things better. He called another monk over, and this monk very studiously set about licking my clit.

It was fantastic. It was the combination of disciplines I suppose. To be taken care of everywhere, it was too good to be true. Everything felt all zingy and crazy and alive. I felt like all the nerve endings in my body were sticking out, erect, craving stimulation.

I don't know where it came from but I couldn't stop myself from shouting out, 'Oh yes, I need to be filled up. I need to be screwed everywhere, by any of you . . .'

The monk who had been licking me pulled away. I groaned desperately. I had been too noisy. Didn't I remember the silence rule?

As I lay there with everything on show, they discussed the proceedings with a cool distance. They rubbed their heads, figuring me out as though I were a mathematical equation. I tried fucking air again. The thing up my arse was wonderful but it was limited. It made me more ready, more susceptible to come, but it didn't tip me over. I was like one of those machines at the amusement arcades. You keep adding two pences because it's almost there, but they never quite slip over. Without more, I would be stuck at 'almost there' forever.

Surely that is the definition of suffering?

Then another monk took his turn. He pulled my labia apart. His thumbs and fingers were bigger than the others, more clumsy, I suppose, but still I welcomed it. I kept saying to myself, 'For fuck's sake, you're lying here surrounded by a bunch of monks with your clit exposed, your cunt wide open and, yes, a fucking great object up your arse!' but the thought only aroused me more.

I was beginning to writhe. I liked the way it looked. It was unspeakably rude. My hips were jerking up and down. A roomful of men were looking at me, looking at what they wanted and couldn't have, well, they could have, but . . .

'Let me suck something . . . a finger or anything,' I moaned. 'Christ, I'm so horny. Can you die from feeling this horny?'

One of the monks reassured me that I couldn't. I just carried on thrusting. I didn't care that there was nothing to thrust against; I had to do the moves, go through the motions, pushing up and down. I was a dirty girl. I couldn't stop myself. It felt so good.

The finger in my mouth moved around my teeth. I could only beg it to do the same down there, between my legs.

Then, heaven, I felt someone's hand on my thigh.

'Yes,' I told whoever it was. 'Do something to me!'

'Shh.'

'For pity's sake, play with me ... I'm begging you. Don't you know anything about compassion?'

'Shut her up,' someone suggested. 'Silence in here.'

A gag was placed over my mouth. Gentle hands held my shoulders but could have been better employed lower down. Different hands pinched my nipples. I hoped I didn't wake up from the pinches. Was this a dream? If it was, I begged myself, whatever you do, don't wake up.

And suddenly I knew, the woman, the woman I had seen at the temple – it was me, or I was the woman. I was trussed up and about to be serviced in exactly the same way as she had been, and I was loving it like she had, and this ... this must be where it all began. My breathing changed as I remembered it all. Oh yes. I was her and she was me and now I knew.

I was going to come whether the final push came or not.

And then I felt someone approach. Finally I was going to have a cock. Someone was preparing themselves, someone was inserting first the head of their cock and then their entire shaft. But it couldn't have been someone because, no, it wasn't attached to anyone. And it vibrated. It had a switch. It vibrated at different speeds. But everyone was watching me; I don't know how many men in robes were watching me now to see how I dealt with this new piece of equipment, this new invasion.

What more could they subject me to?

The speed of my unattached cock increased; my pussy was vibrating, I was vibrating, the whole bloody table was shaking. I had the gag on, but it wouldn't stop me calling out, begging for more, and then I could feel hands on me. Hands on my breasts and, mercifully, hands on my cunt, helping out the mechanical cock, and hands pulling at me as I fought against them, loving the resistance.

And then I was coming, coming all over them, whoever they were, if they were men, monks or machines, I still don't know. I came all over the man attached to my breasts. I came at the man whose tongue was in my mouth. I came with the man whose finger so diligently worked my arse. I came on the man whose tongue slid up and down my clit, and the man who very carefully, very beautifully, fucked me with that extraordinary vibrating cock.

They were all one man.

The next morning, the man in the saffron robe took my hands and examined them. He touched the marks on my wrists and asked, 'Very tender?'

'It's OK.' I smiled. 'When can we do it again?'

'You go tomorrow.'

I couldn't believe it. 'Why? What did I do wrong?'

Had I been too easy? Or too difficult? Was it something to do with my performance or my non-performance? Did they think I wasn't active enough?

'You have to leave tomorrow.'

'I don't want to go. I want to stay here. I want to become a monk and live like you do.'

'It's impossible,' he said calmly. 'Everyone leaves. It is our way.'

'Forget the way,' I pleaded. 'Let's try another way.'

'This is the way,' he said firmly. With the robe swishing around him, as though he were a flickering flame, he stalked away.

The taxi driver was waiting for me. Three mop-haired little boys giggled on the back seats. A small monk with round glasses picked up my rucksack and placed it in the car boot. My bag was heavy but he picked it up as though it was weightless. I sat silently in the passenger seat. I had planned to hide, so they couldn't get rid of me, but a strange acceptance was coming over me. Yes, I had to leave. I couldn't hide here forever. I had to re-enter the real world.

I had to face my demons.

We set off down the mountain. We were only a few hundred yards away when the driver exclaimed loudly. He seemed confused. I looked to see what was upsetting him. We were opposite a beautiful archway. Either side of the arch were trees. Through the golden railings separating that place from the rest of the world I saw groups of Westerners in gowns. I saw monks wandering along. I think some of the monks were chanting. There was a tai-chi class. The students were all in white, bending their knees, stretching and moving their arms in front of their face, like traffic police at a particularly busy junction.

'How can this be?' the driver was saying. He was slapping his hands on the steering wheel.

'What *is* this place?'

The driver didn't know but he thought it might be another monastery. We drove nearer. The sign said,

HERE, ALL YOUR DESIRES WILL EVAPORATE AND YOU
WILL TREAD THE PATH TO ENLIGHTENMENT.

I didn't understand it. How could there be two of
these places so close together? If this was the one the
guidebooks all talked about then what in hell was the
other place?

The taxi driver was reluctant but I insisted he drove
me back to the first place. I had this weird feeling that
we might go back there and find nothing. That it would
have disappeared, leaving me to wonder whether it was
all just a dream, like in the stories I used to write as a
kid: '. . . and then Lauren woke up in her bed.' Then
there would be a small clue leaving you to just wonder:
'Hmm, did that really happen or not?'

But there was nothing so ambiguous when we got
back to the first monastery. It *was* still there and everything was exactly the same, except that this time I
noticed that outside the gate there was a small sign
partially obscured by some brambles.

'Stop the car,' I said. I got out and walked towards
the sign. I had to push the leaves aside to read it. Clearly
no one had bothered with it for years. It read, HERE,
ALL YOUR DESIRES WILL BE FULFILLED.

The taxi driver bit his lip. His face was white. He
looked afraid. He knew his mistake and so did I.

'You want me take you to the other place now?'

I got into the passenger seat and slammed the door.
Even the little kids in the back seat had long stopped
giggling.

'No, that's quite all right,' I said. 'I've had enough
enlightenment to last me a lifetime.'

14

I had to go to see Callum. I was ready for it now. I went to The Everest and marched up to the man with the caterpillar moustache.

'I'm back!' He didn't raise his head as he told me, 'You're too late. He's gone!'

I could hear 'And So Sally Can't Wait' bleeding through his headphones.

'What? Well, maybe he just went for a walk?'

'No,' said the receptionist smugly. You could tell he enjoyed being the bearer of bad news. 'He paid. He's not coming back.'

Callum had checked out? Where did he go? I knew he must have left a message or something for me.

'No message,' said the man as though he were reading my mind.

I felt uncomfortable being there now, so I moved next door to Les Trois Peaks. It was more expensive than The Everest but I was just glad to have somewhere convenient to go. I supposed that Chelle was back and that Callum was with her. I hoped he might come looking for me, but I didn't think he would.

I was lucky. I met a couple of Australian girls in the reception area and they decided to adopt me. Merry and Kim had been backpacking in India and were staying in Kathmandu for a week before moving on to Tibet. They thought they might get an audience with the Dalai Lama. Merry was a journalist. I didn't find out what Kim did. I told them that I had been on a trek and I told them that one member of our party had become sick and I had stepped in to help. I told them about the storm and being buried in a tent for three days and how scary it had been.

'You're really kind,' they said. 'You must be so nice giving up your place to nurse somebody.' That made me feel guilty but not guilty enough to tell them how I felt about that member of our party, or what my nursing had involved. There were some things I drew the line at, however much I wanted to share it with someone. It was hard to be admired when I so blatantly didn't deserve it.

I didn't tell them about the monastery either. Not because they wouldn't have appreciated it, I'm sure it was right up their street, but I just couldn't bare to go into the details. They might ask, 'How did you let it happen?' and I wasn't sure I could answer that yet.

Anyway, Merry and Kim were party girls. They could sniff a party from miles away; they had some kind of good-times radar, so the first night I found myself in Ye Olde Teapot, a bar packed with Antipodeans. The pictures on the walls and the mirrors behind the bar somehow reminded me of O'Harts.

I have to explain something. This thing I had for Callum, infatuation, obsession, love, whatever you want to call it, was not the usual me. I was not one to mope. I wasn't the nostalgic type. Back home, when my friends had signed up to websites to get in touch with all their old mates, I laughed.

'You mean Wankers Reunited?' I said. 'What's the point? There's no going back. Look on. Look forwards. Don't you know we're in the middle of a population explosion? The planet is literally bursting with gorgeous young men who want to fuck you! Why fuck someone you've done it with before? You obviously didn't like them enough back then, otherwise you'd still be with them, so why would you like them more now?'

When they said that there were reunions, I said that it was just a chance to show-off or to humiliate, or at least to slip into the comfortable old roles they'd had at school.

For sixteen years I succeeded in putting Callum out of my head. I think you do that quite easily when you've been let down like I had. You don't let yourself dwell on bad staff. The people who were most anxious about the past were the ones who thought they had made the mistakes. They were the ones it hurt the most. They were the ones who were stuck in the per-haps-he-was-right-for-me loop and they just didn't real-ise it. The ones who made the decisions suffered the self-doubt. I didn't get to make the decisions, so in the end I didn't have to suffer.

Callum had betrayed me, so I wasn't going to go crawling back to him.

Well, that was the plan.

On the second night, when the Australian girls knocked for me to 'come out to play', I was less keen. I still had a raging headache from the previous night and I wasn't sure I wanted to spoil another day. In the morning, Nepal was at its best. Before eleven, the air wasn't polluted by the smog, the children danced through the streets with their arms full of schoolbooks, the women carried out their chores in saris of all the glorious colours of the earth and some that seemed not of this world. I also surmised that if Callum did come for me then he might come in the morning. I don't know why, but I just thought he would. Morning is, after all, a most innocent time of day, so if he told Chelle he was going to see me in the morning then she could hardly object. It seemed a sacrifice to give that up but Merry and Kim were pretty persuasive, and I suppose I was pretty persuadable.

According to Merry and Kim there were no hot men in Ye Olde Teapot, nor in Hilary's Hut. The Third Eye was too expensive. Still, we had a drink, maybe two or three, in each of the bars, so that by the time we walked into The Third Way I was steaming.

'There are no hot men anywhere,' I argued but, with the aid of beer goggles, the men were distinctly warming up. Merry and Kim were a lot more sober than I was, but even they wobbled into each other.

The first thing I saw as we walked in was the sign: NEPAL'S FIRST EVER WET T-SHIRT CONTEST. Actually, there wasn't a Nepalese in sight. That club was wall to wall with Westerners. Western *men*, that is.

'Look at that,' I said. My voice sounded squeaky. I heard Merry, or was it Kim, say, 'Shi-it!'

'Girls! Welcome!' The bar manager was over at us, rubbing his hands. 'So glad you could come. Let's go round the back and get you ready.'

'Shall we?' Merry and Kim looked at each other.

I burped. 'Do we get free drinks?'

'Baby,' the man said, 'the whole night is on me.'

'Well, in that case –' I checked to see if Merry and Kim were in accord, '– we're in!'

'Are there any other contestants?' Merry asked.

'Yup,' he said, 'but they're not half as well stacked as you three.'

'Who's the judge?' I asked. I was so drunk that I wasn't sure if I had actually spoken.

'I am.'

I don't know how it happened but somehow I got

separated from Merry and Kim, and I ended up in the back room where the other contestants were getting ready or, as the manager said, 'Putting on their make-up and doing those things you girlies do.'

There were four girls in there. They looked miserable. Even if they had tits like Pamela Anderson, their expressions would have let them down.

'OK, take your tops off. No bras please. Put on the T-shirts.'

The T-shirts were sitting in a bowl of warm water. I pulled one out. On the back it said, 'I like to take it up The Third Way.' On the front it said, 'Play with my Nepals.'

'Very funny,' I said, pulling it on. The other girls wouldn't meet my eye.

'You look gorgeous,' said the manager. I got the idea that I was his designated favourite.

When I saw the state of the others in their wet T-shirts, I thought I might actually win. The girls seemed to divide into big (but in which case they were droopy) or pert, but on the small side. Maybe mine – which were big but still fairly upstanding – might do the trick.

The manager certainly seemed to think so.

I looked up at him. He was smiling salaciously at me. He was a big, bald man who was so fucking sexy my nipples were saluting him. If I hadn't just been shagged to within an inch of my life at the monastery, and if the love of my life hadn't just disappeared to God-knows-where, then I definitely might have considered inviting him back.

Or inviting him up, to put it another way.

'You're going to win, babe,' he said, and I realised that it wasn't a confidence-booster but that he had decided that I *was* going to win. Nevertheless, he still tweaked my breasts for good luck. He pushed me against a wall. I was so drunk that I just kind of flopped there.

'You'll never guess where I've just been,' I murmured. I was going to tell him about my last night at the monastery and what it feels like to orgasm in a room crowded with monks. Or I could have told him how it feels to make love to the man of your dreams pretending to be his wife. But I didn't get the words out.

The manager had pushed up my T-shirt and was now rubbing his face in my tits. My breasts loved it, even if I was a little shocked. He had a great big hard-on straining against his pants. I pushed him away. Yes, I may have been pissed but I wasn't stupid.

I remember a beach with Callum. We were going to split in one month but I didn't know that at the time. The tide was coming in. You could hear the sound of the water slapping on the sand. I was holding a shell to my ear.

'I don't hear anything.'

Callum put the shell to his ear; 'Really? Well, I can hear loads of things.'

'Liar.' I tried to grab the shell out of his hand but he held it out of my reach. He was teasing me. He loved teasing me.

'No, *you* are. I'll never lie to you,' Callum said, suddenly serious. 'Ask me anything; I'll prove it.'

'What shall I ask?'

'Ask me if I love you!'

I laughed. 'I hope I know the answer to that. Let's try a more difficult question. OK, do you think I'm beautiful?'

'I think you're incredibly sexy.'

'But not beautiful?'

Why couldn't he lie? Why couldn't he tell me I was even if he didn't think so? Didn't he know how that would please me?

'You're not classically beautiful,' he said, and the annoying thing was he was really thinking about this carefully. 'But I think you're lovely.'

That was the best I was going to get.

He put his hand between my legs. There was no hesitation or question about it. He was free to touch me as though I was a part of him. He touched me as he might scratch an itch. I was wearing denim shorts. He loved these shorts. He said they drove him wild. He was telling the truth. We drove each other wild. That was what we did. There were other people on the beach but they didn't know that he was rubbing me there. Callum never lied.

When they said that I was the winner of the Kathmandu Miss Wet T-shirt contest I was more embarrassed than anything. Well, I was flattered too, of course, but I knew that my tits were pretty good anyway. I didn't really need a trophy to tell me that.

'Oh shit,' I said to Merry. 'What the fuck do I have to do now?'

'Go and get the prize.'

I had to walk across the bar. Then I had to choose a song.

'I have to dance?'

'Only if you want,' the manager said. He had moved on to another of the contestants. His hand disappeared down the back of the girl's shorts. 'But I don't think the crowd will like it if you walk out on them.'

'Oh.' I looked at the big butch hiking types who made up the crowd.

How quickly alcohol wears off sometimes.

When I started moving to the music, though, the crowd clapped along and, after a few seconds, I realised I felt good up there. As I danced, my skirt flipped and whirled at my thighs. Everyone was looking up my legs. I was wearing snow boots up to my knee but my thighs felt gloriously on show. Plus, there were my tits showing through the T-shirt as though there was no material between me and everyone there at all.

Some of the men stretched up their hands to me and I offered a hand down to them. I was loving it. I hardly cared if the men enjoyed it or not. I relaxed like I was alone in my bedroom, about to go out on a hot date. I was so relaxed that I undid my skirt. It fell to the floor with a whoop from the crowd that was just unbelievable. I was just in my boots, knickers and this wet T-shirt. I felt like a queen. That is, if a queen ever stood half-naked at a bar gyrating to 'You Can Leave Your Hat On' then she would feel like this.

It was the perfect song to dance to. I looked out into the audience, catching the eyes of some of the men. I let my hair wash over my face. I felt so sexy, sexier than I had felt in a long time; 10,000 monks can't be wrong, I thought. This was incredibly easy too. The ease with which I did it made it seem right. It also made me think about the temple. I thought about the face of that one woman tied up, surrounded, with no escape. I knew how that felt now. I made my face like hers. I swung my body like I thought she would move hers. I hooked my fingers in my knickers. I was sure I looked amazing. I was born to do this.

I imagined they were a room full of Callums and they were all gagging for me.

And then I saw him. Callum really was there. My Callum. He was fully dressed and his hair was freshly washed. He looked perfectly normal apart from the fact that he must have been about 12 pounds lighter than he was when I first saw him in the Kathmandu street. His T-shirt was hanging off his shoulders and his jeans looked about to slip down. I don't think he was gagging for me though. If there's a reverse of gagging for someone then that pretty much describes the way Callum looked as he pushed through the crowds towards me.

He stood at the bottom of the stage, then grabbed my wrist and pretty much pulled me off. The audience booed him, but only half-heartedly since the song was ending anyway. By the time the next song started and the girl who came second – the girl who was now first in the manager's books – leaped up to take my place, the crowd had forgotten me.

'Callum,' I roared. I knew it was important to get the first word in but it was hard to compete with the noise in that room. 'What the hell are you doing here? You should be in bed.'

'Too right! He can be in my bed any time,' I could hear Merry saying.

And then Kim said, 'Cor! He's fit! She didn't tell us that!'

Callum didn't say anything yet. Instead, he gripped me by the elbows and steered me back through the crowds. Where did he get his strength from?

'How did you find me?' I burbled incoherently. I didn't want him to get the chance to speak. He looked like he was going to kill me. 'I was just dancing for the crowd and . . .'

'I guessed!' he hissed. 'You . . . you . . . how dare you?'

'What do you mean? I won the competition and it was part of my . . . my duties, you see, and . . .'

Callum was frightening me. Perhaps this was part of

his illness. He had had the shortness of breath and the skin pale enough to frighten a ghost and now he had a kind of murderous madness about him.

I wondered if the manager would rescue me. Somehow I doubted it. He was too busy with girl number two. Besides, he would probably rescue my tits but be quite glad to leave the rest of me behind.

'I don't mean that!' Callum's look proclaimed I was the most stupid woman he had ever had the misfortune to meet.

'Then ... what?'

'You fucked me!'

'Sorry? Callum, I don't get you.'

He backed me to the edge of the room. The crowd was all facing the girl on the bar and so no one noticed me, or saw the difficulty I was in. I have to admit, that girl was pretty good. I think she might have been a professional from the way she slid up and down the pole. For the first time, I got what pole-dancing was all about.

'I'll get my friends. They'll tell you. It was just a competition.'

Callum slapped my arse. 'Listen to me, for fuck's sake.'

'I am,' I pleaded.

'You've been fucking me behind my back!'

If it weren't so awful it would have been funny. I picked up a drink. At the same time, Callum shoved me backwards so I was right against the wall. A picture of a mandala slipped behind me and vodka spilled all over my T-shirt (not that it wasn't sopping wet already).

'I don't know what you mean,' I protested. Fuck! Callum really was taking the whole thing very seriously.

'Yes, you do.'

'How could I fuck you without ... without you knowing?'

'You pretended to be Chelle so that you could have your way with me. You're wicked!'

'No, Callum, you were delirious, sick. You didn't know what was happening. You must have dreamt –'

'Stop lying to me, you little sexy, gorgeous, wild darling.'

Callum grabbed me around the middle and swung me around. I couldn't believe it. I kicked a guy as I went around, apologised and then pushed my head into Callum's shoulders. I couldn't believe it.

'You haven't changed, Lauren, you know that? Sixteen years and you haven't changed a bit. You're as cheeky as ever!'

Callum knew. He knew. And he didn't mind. This was better than anything I could have dreamt up. I kept slapping his shoulder blades and then holding him to me. I felt his breath next to me. His chest pressed against mine. It was wonderful. I bit his shoulder. He pushed me away, but gently, just so that he could kiss me properly. His lips were so perfect on mine; I swooned. There, right there, in the middle of The Third Way, with my sopping wet T-shirt on, I swooned. I thought I might come.

'Hmm, or maybe you have. You're a little bigger than before, I think.'

Callum was feeling my tits; mine, not Chelle's. He wanted *me*. Then he pulled me over to the seating area, where it was much quieter and quite a bit darker. There were just a few hippies in there, smoking grass and pouring wax on to the back of their hands. It was like a different place. The music from the bar came over like a distant crackle of a radio.

'Let me have a good look at you then.'

'Not here.' I couldn't believe him. And he had called *me* cheeky.

'Yes, here. Look, you shouldn't wear wet clothes. It's not good for you; you'll catch a cold. Let me take it off for you. That's right.'

He pulled my T-shirt over my shoulders and we let it fall to the floor. He put his hands on my tits. He dropped to his knees and then he put his face between them like the manager had done; only the back of my Callum's head was beautiful. I could have held his head there for the rest of my life. Then he pinched my nipple between his lips, looked up at me and winked. It was amazing. I groaned. I couldn't help it. I let out a big loud greedy groan, right there in the shadows of the club. But then I remembered.

'Where's Chelle?'

'Your guess is as good as mine,' he murmured, and then he crammed more of my breasts in his mouth. He didn't want to talk about Chelle, I realised, but then neither did I. Why spoil the fun? Then he pulled away and whispered into my mouth.

'These titties are a lot bigger than they used to be. What did you do? Implants?' He squeezed them between his lips tighter. He was a fucking glutton!

'Nah, they just grew. It was from all that massage you used to give me.'

'Fucking hell, Lauren.'

Lauren. He said my name!

I pulled him up to kiss me but, although he kissed me passionately, I could feel his attention was wandering to my breasts again. He wouldn't keep away from them. I mean, he really wanted to be there, he was mad for my nipples. He kept shoving them in those wonderful heart-shaped lips of his and rolling them around and around his tongue.

I was wearing next to nothing and he was all wrapped up warm.

No one was looking, but who cared if they were?

'Let's get these panties out of the way,' Callum said. I tugged at the sides of my knickers and when I reached my knees he said, 'Stop.'

Fuck, I loved him for remembering that. He hadn't forgotten what I liked. Perhaps he never would.

'You've been trimming.'

'Well, people didn't do that in the eighties.'

'Come on, show me what you've got.'

I tucked my fingers down. Then I stopped. Could we really do that here? Then I put my finger in his mouth so it was wet, and then I was opening my slit out to him. We were old friends. There was nothing to be afraid of. He was with me now. Me.

'OK?'

'More than OK,' he whispered. 'That's right, rub yourself, babe. You always were the naughtiest girl in the school.'

I had finally managed to get his attention away from my titties. He positioned himself lower on the floor to get a better look at my crack. He was just looking. I don't know if anyone else could see us or not. I didn't care; I started to thrust and wriggle into his face. I felt so horny. It was a combination of winning the contest, the dancing and everything else, I suppose. I wanted him to look up my cunt and to crawl right inside me. This was all I needed; this, and a long hard screw. (But I wouldn't have said no to a quick hard one either.)

Eventually, other boys asked me out. You would be shocked how many of them did. I think it was because they could tell I wasn't a virgin. You didn't go out with a type like Callum and get to 'protect your inner sanctum'.

That much was obvious. But I needed Callum's form of love and sunshine. The guys who called were too like me, brooding and sullen; I needed something different. I hated the men when they called yet I hated them when they didn't. They couldn't do a thing right, but I guess I never made that clear because they all seemed to think I loved them madly.

Since Callum and I split, I have had seven lovers and three long-term relationships. This is what I tell people. That is the official figure. In reality, I have had twenty-four lovers and five long-term relationships.

You do the maths.

There was Harry, who took me to a cottage in the Lake District and made me watch porno videos. We watched them back to back. We lay on the floor and fucked in front of them. For a time I thought I wouldn't be able to have sex without a porno video in the same room. I loved watching the women with their arched backs and the way they threw back their hair with such abandonment. I loved that the women were so much better looking than the men. It made it all so sordid, so seedy. It was like the women would have sex with anyone, just because they wanted to have sex.

There was Peter. My friends called him 'Peter the Virgin' because, well, because he was. He was waiting for the right woman, but he met me first. Seducing him was a serious business and it was a joy. I had never understood those people who say that the chase is everything, but with Pete it must have been because the day after we had sex, terrific, heartbreaking sex, I decided I never wanted to see him again.

There was Saul, who liked me to be dressed up to the nines or 'dressed up to the sixty-nines', as he said. Callum used to like me in sexy underwear but Saul's choices weren't sexy. They were bizarre. It took me half an hour to put on the red rubber catsuit and when I took it off my body was stained bright red. Saul also liked masked sex; he would spring out at me from the wardrobe and have me on his cold wooden floorboards or he would spy on me in the bathroom and then make me dress in PVC shorts and walk all over him. On the tiles. This was before the days of an Ann Summers in every high street and I had to use a mail order catalogue to get the gear. The worst thing was that whereas I would be dressed in all this finery, Saul would be wearing baggy boxer shorts. Sometimes these shorts had a print on them of Christmas trees or Mickey Mouse. In the end I decided Saul wasn't making much of an effort and, besides, the sex wasn't as much fun as the outfits were.

There was Thomas, who wanted me to fight when we fucked. He would pin me down and bite me and I would have to rip his back with my nails. He wanted me to grow my nails long and paint them red. I managed an inch before I could hardly use my computer. I doubted Thomas and I would last as long as my nail varnish.

'How close pleasure is to pain,' he used to say virtually each time we got together. 'They are like brother and sister.'

'Like a brother and sister who hate each other very much!' I retorted.

This leads me conveniently on to Keith. Keith was perfect in nearly every way. He was kind and funny. He had a great job, he was great in bed. He was handsome. It was the 2 per cent of him that wasn't perfect that buggered us. His 2 per cent was simply unforgivable. You see, Keith had an equally perfect sister, Cassandra. Like him, she had a great job, was beautiful, clever, funny. Once, I went to his home unexpectedly and found them unexpectedly entwined. In bed. With no clothes on.

'How do you know they were doing anything?' an overly optimistic friend asked. And I didn't know *for sure* if anything was going on. But I knew near enough.

By then, it didn't have to be delivered to me on a plate.

Back at Les Trois Peaks, Callum walked agitatedly around the room. He was about to tell me something. I lay on the bed and waited. I knew what he was about to say was important to him, but I had no idea what it could be.

Finally, he found the words. 'Lauren, you've been so naughty. I'm afraid I'm going to have to punish you.'

'No, you're not,' I said, but I said it weakly because I couldn't imagine anything in the world better than Callum's punishment. There was certainly nothing I wanted more.

He tied my arms together with socks and then he covered my eyes with a T-shirt. So far so good.

'I didn't know what was going on – and now you don't. Isn't that fair?'

'OK,' I said. I tried to sound casual about it, but inside I was squirming; Callum, you devil. You *have* changed, but it's all good!

First he made me lean over the bed. I suppose I could have fought him off, but what would have been the point? I loved it. Each thwack on my arse made me quiver. I knew he could see my cunt and I wanted him to see it. Did the sight of my red oval, the curling hairs, excite him? It certainly excited me to show him. I was filled with wetness.

More slapping. It hurt. This wasn't like the good old days.

He threw me on the bed and I thought we were going to make love but he put his cock in my mouth. Then he took it out. I didn't know when it was going to come back to me. And I was desperate. I could only imagine how sexy it must look. I was sticking out my tongue, pursing my lips, waiting for the sweet hardness of his cock. Then he moved around the room. I strained to hear what was coming my way. Sometimes, his lips were on me. Sometimes his tongue would flicker around my teeth. I couldn't wait.

Then he tied my legs up too. They were too far apart for comfort really. I could feel the insides of my thighs start to ache. I thought of the monks but I preferred this. This was with my man.

'Please do it now,' I begged.

'What did you say?'

'I said give me it!'

'How do I know you really are Lauren?'

'It is me. It is!' I said desperately, fucking the air. 'Look at me!'

I could sense him examining me down there. It was amazing. 'Please touch me,' I said, 'then you'll know it's me!'

He slid a finger into me and said, 'Hmm, it certainly feels like Lauren.'

Then, very slowly and very deliberately, he licked me and said, 'And you certainly taste like Lauren.'

'Callum, no one wants you like I want you.'

'That may be true,' he said. His cock slid into me. I had to take sharp intakes of breath. It was so big and ready. And I was so spread, so wide open to him. I wanted to wrap my legs around him but I couldn't, so I railed against the strings that kept me back. I could still move my pelvis though and I thrust as much as I could until I could feel him deeper and deeper. He was getting faster and more desperate and I was too.

His breath was hot in my ear. He licked around me there and I kept my mouth open for his tongue.

'But do you fuck like Lauren?' he said.

'Oh yes,' I told him. 'I'll show you.'

I pushed and thrust and wriggled with all my might, and I clenched too, so that his cock would feel like it never wanted to leave. I could hear this animal moaning and didn't realise at first that it was me and then, just as I thought I couldn't take any more of it, he sucked long and hard on my nipples and I couldn't hold back any more.

Callum and I lay curled up in each other. 'You've got beautiful hair,' he said.

'It's not *that* beautiful,' I said.

He gave me this kind of sad smile and then nuzzled my ear. His lips wrapped around me and I could feel the tug straight in my cunt.

'So when did you first realise it was me?'

'Guess.'

'The last night, when we ... er ... you know ...'

'When I fucked your tight little arsehole and you screamed blue murder? They could have heard you in China.'

'Well, you were pumping me so hard I thought I was going to end up in China. OK, if not then ... was it the first time I let you put your finger up there?'

'You mean the time you said you didn't want it, and then you did? You really did. You loved it, didn't you? I've never felt a pussy that wet and tight before. It wasn't then though. Guess again.'

'OK. Was it the time with the blindfold?'

'The time you sat on me, you cheeky cow, when you nearly drowned me in your pussy? Not that I'm complaining. No, it wasn't then. Try again.'

'Not the first time? The time I gave you a blow job?'

'Yeah,' Callum started laughing.

I wasn't sure that he was telling the truth but I jumped on him and shouted, 'You let me think you didn't know? I can't believe you did that to me! Do you know how bad I felt?'

But I didn't feel bad any more. That was then and this was now. Callum moved down to my tits. He caught my nipple between his teeth and it made me sigh like a fool. 'You've got quite a distinctive blow-job style.'

'What do you mean?'

'Put it this way – no one licks my balls like you do.' He smiled at me with such affection in his eyes that I felt tears spring to mine. 'You poor guilty thing, you really had no idea that I knew?'

'Nope. Not at all. Well, at least I can be myself now.'

'Ooh,' he said smugly. 'I think I saw pretty much the real you up there on the mountainside.'

I was triumphant. 'Babe, you ain't seen nothing yet. And you certainly haven't heard what I can do.'

After we had made love again, roaring out each other's names, I finally asked Callum the question I had been waiting to ask ever since he came to find me. The crazy thing was I didn't really care about Chelle now. All I really wanted to know about was Rose Connelly. I had to have my answer. I couldn't pretend everything was fine any longer. It may have been history but history never goes away.

'Callum, did you ever love me?'

He looked away, then he groaned and sank his head

in the pillow. I couldn't read his actions at all. I had lost that confidence.

'You *must* know the answer to that.'

'I thought I did,' I admitted, 'but then everything changed. What about you and Rose? Will you tell me what happened?'

Callum looked like the mattress had suddenly sprung up hundreds of rusty nails. He spoke slowly. 'I still think back to then and think why did I have to do that? Why did I have to be so stupid?'

I could feel the disappointment shudder deep down within me. I was right all along. I had hoped I was wrong and that there was a mistake, but my head *had* known the truth.

'Oh well, we all do stupid things when we're young,' I muttered. 'I can't say I was perfectly innocent either.' I got up to look out the window. Outside, in the back yard, they were chasing chickens. Later they would be slaughtered and thrown into boiling pans. We would eat chicken curry tonight.

So he hadn't even denied it.

About a week after Callum and I split, I went to O'Harts. It was a Thursday – an evening I knew Callum wouldn't be there. Thursday night was textile night or something at art college. Dave was there, though, as always. He ignored me in the pub all night except to ask me why I had come. When he left I followed him out in the street and told him that I fancied him. He didn't say anything at first. He just looked me up and down with his cold green eyes. He had been in a fight a few days previously and his left cheek was still purple and angry. I thought he was going to spit at me or walk away or something. Instead he pinned me against the wall and ripped my shirt open. I was stood there in the middle of the street with my tits hanging out. My nipples were little bullets waiting for his tongue. He was a nasty sod. I knew it and he knew it. He didn't care about me, but it worked me up more than I care to admit. It was just the place I wanted it to happen; it was how I wanted it. It was just the way I had seen him take other girls; other faceless, anonymous girls he didn't care about. A car went by and I heard people shout and it was probably something at us, or me. It was probably something like 'slapper' or 'slag', but I was glued to the spot. I was so turned on I couldn't speak. He pulled my knickers to one side. He didn't even bother taking them down, but it wasn't in the way Callum would leave my knickers on, because Dave really didn't care. That was clear. He fingered me casually and then he undid his pants and straightened his cock – he didn't need my help, thank you – and shoved it up me.

I tried to remember to breathe.

'Fuck! You're a tight bitch, aren't you?' he said. He didn't have to say Callum's name. Callum's name was always there around us. 'Now I can see why he went for you.'

He pushed himself in and out of me, and I knew it was all for his benefit, not mine. He kept my arms behind my back in a lock like he was a policeman and I was his prisoner. He fucked me hard the way they fuck in porno films, but worse because he didn't kiss but sucked hard at my neck. I was afraid he would bite me and maybe draw blood.

'He didn't want to share you with anyone. He'll be so fucked up when he finds out about this,' he said spitefully.

I hated Dave. I let his mouth come down to my tits

and I felt like he swallowed me up whole. It was all for his pleasure, but somehow that gave me freedom to do what I wanted.

I tore my arm free and pulled his head closer to me, made him force my tits down his mouth.

'You love it, don't you?' he snarled in my ear. 'A bit of rough. You dirty slag.'

Anyone walking along that street would have seen what we were doing. They would have seen his white buttocks working in and out, swooping in and out of me and forcing me against the wall. And they would hear my moans of pleasure even though I bit his collar because I didn't want him to hear me groan. I didn't want him to think I was actually enjoying it. I remember thinking, textile night at the college.

'You're a dirty slag. You'll fuck anyone. You can't get enough of it, can you?' he went on.

He was grunting and swearing and fucking me with all his might and each shunt pushed me up so my feet lost contact with the ground and the back of my head bounced against the wall and my whole body pushed against him. Yet, by doing that, I was getting into a rhythm with him, fucking him hard. I wouldn't give him the satisfaction of showing my enjoyment, except I was nearly there. I was nearly, yes, I was coming all over him.

Then he pulled himself out and shoved me down to him. He was huge and glistening, a great purple head with my juices on him.

'Suck it, bitch!' he said. And when I thought my jaw would break he hissed, 'I'm going to come all over your face.'

He did and I licked it off. He zipped up his flies and left. Dave was no Callum. I knew that then, but I didn't care. I wanted to dig deep into the heart of Callum. And Dave was willing to be the scalpel.

Callum asked me to sit down. I couldn't get back into the bed. I said, 'I'm not annoyed.' I guess he knew from that how annoyed I really was. 'I shouldn't have asked.' My voice was shaky. 'It just hurts, even now after all this time.'

Callum looked at me like he'd just picked up a rock and found a thousand creepy-crawlies writhing underneath. He said quietly, 'I hate myself for hurting you.'

'Do you mind . . . telling me how it happened?'

He nodded. He began uncertainly. I was amazed that he would talk about it and I wasn't sure that I really wanted to hear. But I let him speak.

'Rose picked something for herself, and I picked something for you. It just seemed like a good idea to nick stuff as both of us were skint at the time and no one seemed to care. I wouldn't have taken from any of the small shops. We only used the large stores, the . . .'

I had to stop him there. 'That's not all you did? Shoplifting?'

He looked at me strangely. 'Yes it is. Why do you say that?'

How ludicrous an image that really was. Him and Rose roaming through department stores and slipping bits and bobs up their jumpers. Don't make me laugh, I thought.

'Oh, come on. Why are you treating me like an idiot? You went thieving with Rose? You would have been better off by yourself. There would have been less chance of getting caught.'

'She helped me.' He blushed. He was so red that you could barely distinguish his lips from his cheeks. 'She helped me choose things you would like. I didn't know what you wanted. What did I know? Rose got it spot-on every time. Rose really looked up to you. Don't try and tell me the presents weren't always perfect. I just wanted to make you happy. I know it sounds mad but I thought you would go off me unless I did something memorable. You were so happy that Christmas, and I wanted to make you happy always.'

His gifts were, without fail, fabulous. They were always the right size yet he never hassled me for my size. They were always the right colour as though intuitively he understood what would suit me. He never asked me in advance if I wanted something but would roll up with something I didn't know I wanted until I had it.

And that was all because of Rose?

'I still –' I couldn't begin to get my head around the idea. 'You *were* screwing her though, as well as all that, weren't you?'

'Screwing her? Rose Connelly? You thought that's what I was doing?'

'Ye-es.'

'You thought I would be unfaithful?'

'Uh huh, well . . .'

'I would never –' he said, and then he paused. He registered the situation and so did I. I got to say it first.

'Well, you are now.'

'This is different. This is you. I would never let you down. Not now. Not then.' Callum turned around and made me face him. 'You know, I never got over that, especially the way you fucked me and left me. How did you think I felt?'

'I didn't think how you felt. I just thought . . .'

I still couldn't believe it. I was sure he and Rose were

having sex. How could Rose not have fancied Callum? How could he not have wanted Rose?

'Dave *told* me you were with her.'

'But he was an idiot. You knew that. Lauren, you really humiliated me,' Callum went on. 'You made me feel so small. How could you have done that?'

'I'm sorry.'

'Sorry is not good enough. So what were you going to tell me?'

'Nothing!'

'Yes, you were. You said you weren't entirely innocent.'

'It's all in the past.'

'You're the one who wouldn't let go of the past. Not me. Now tell me what you were going to say or I leave.'

Callum got up. He pulled his T-shirt over his head. I felt sick with fear. He was going to walk out on me after all this!

'I slept with Dave,' I said uselessly. I don't know why I said it, and if I could unsay it, even now, I would. I should have lied. Nothing could have prepared me for the look of horror on his face. He looked like he was going to throw up.

'Dave-Dave?'

'Ye-es,' I said, as though Dave-Dave explained everything. I wished it did.

'He told me.' Callum was shaking his head. He looked like he had when he was up the mountains. There was no colour in his face now. The blood had all drained away. 'Dave told me that once but I refused to believe it. Why would I believe that? We had a fight. We both ended up in A and E. I never spoke to him again. I stopped going to O'Harts. I lost all my mates. That's why I moved away. I had no friends in town any more.

I met Chelle and she helped me get a job and ... but fucking hell, Lauren, why Dave?'

'I don't know.'

I thought about the wasted years. The years I had been confused or screwed up just because of this. No, it was just because of me, jumping to stupid conclusions. It was crazy, it really was. It was like I was going back to somewhere I knew but finding everything was different. It wasn't just as if the old cinema had been pulled down and turned into a fancy café, but as if I had just found out that the old cinema had also been doubling as a museum or a casino all that time.

Callum fucked me hard, harder than he had ever fucked me before. I cried out, and I was thinking of all the times we could have been doing this and we weren't. Stupid fucking Rose. Stupid fucking Callum. We were both so angry. We were both so pent up. I had never felt this furious before. But I don't think we were enraged with each other; I think we were both damning the situation. But I was furious with myself too for responding in this way, for the way my legs wrapped around Callum. For the way I was encouraging him on, and after I had stopped telling him to get off me, I told him to get deeper, harder, faster.

'Oh Christ, Callum, this is unbelievable.'

I cried out things that in the cold light of day would be too embarrassing to repeat, too sentimental or too horny. I was screaming, 'Don't ever leave me.'

'You want it, don't you?'

'Stay inside me,' I insisted, and his mouth was on my tits as he screwed me so tightly I thought I would explode.

'Pump me,' I demanded.

'You like it like this, don't you?'

'I do, yes, I do. I want it good and hard.'

I slapped his buttocks, driving him inside me like I was whipping a horse; 'Come on. Faster. Harder. Don't stop.'

At some point Callum's ring, his white gold Russian wedding ring, must have fallen off. We found it later on the floor just under the bed, in a pool of dust and fluff. It must have been too big for him now that he had lost weight. Even his fingers were a different size. But I saw it as something more meaningful than that, though. Well, you would, wouldn't you? Surely it was a sign.

15

The sun streamed in. It was the perfect day for some sightseeing and shopping. The crazy city had been awake long before us. We could hear the cry of the market traders intermingled with the chorus of the birds. The wind was up; it made our curtains dance.

Callum went down to reception to use the phone. It felt like he was gone ages but I suppose it could only have been a minute or two at the most. I missed him from the moment he said he was going. I suddenly felt very tiny in the bed.

When Callum came back, he was spitting fire. For a moment I thought, Gosh, he looks quite funny when he's angry.

'The ... that bitch. She's not coming back yet. She and Stella have gone off to Chitwan.'

'What's that?'

'The national safari park. She knew I wanted to go there. She *knew* it. It was the only reason I agreed to come to this godforsaken dump in the first place.'

I hated it when he spoke like that about Nepal. Wasn't he glad he came? Didn't he remember the beauty of it? Most of all, wasn't he glad he found me again?

'Chelle said that I'm out of danger but I still need to rest so there's no point in rushing back for nothing. Rushing back for nothing? She's my wife for God's sake. She's meant to want to be with me!'

So what was I meant to do? Look sad? Commiserate?

I did try, but my joy at this turn of events was too great to hide. The longer Chelle was away, the longer this mouse could play. And I knew that with just a little more time I could make it impossible for Callum to leave me. I knew too that Chelle probably was just having a high old time with Stella. They were probably licking and sucking and fucking all over the place. She *was* a bitch – far more even than Callum knew.

'What if Chelle has met someone else?' I asked. I couldn't help myself. Callum started pulling off his clothes again. Hurray! He kicked off his shoes. He was getting back in bed with me. I had been afraid he was going to demand some 'thinking' time alone!

'She wouldn't. She definitely wouldn't.' He slid in next to me. His fingers were cold on my waist. He pushed his cock against my arse. Delicious! I had a feeling Chelle wasn't really on his mind right now.

'Poor Callum,' I said. 'I'll have to look after you for a little longer then.'

'Come here,' he said. 'I need your medicine.' He pulled me on top of him. Before I could say, 'Don't ever come back, Chelle,' Callum had his hands on my tits and was releasing my nipples from the bra. I straddled him, my legs either side of his body. I bounced up and down on him. I was laughing, bobbing up and down. I couldn't pretend to be sad that Chelle wasn't coming back! Ring out the bells!

'Hey, baby,' I sang, 'we don't have to take our clothes off . . .'

But Callum silenced me with his kisses. 'But it helps if we do!'

I pushed him down and held his arms over his head. He wasn't going to get away from me. I felt his cock rise up me. He put his fingers to my clit and smiled up at me.

'Come on, baby, what are you waiting for? Aren't you going to fuck me?'

'Oh yes, I'm going to fuck you,' I told him, and already I was moving up and down on him. Raising my buttocks off and on, pushing down on to him and clenching him inside me.

'Oh yes, oh yes, oh yes.'

Everything else could be forgotten. All the past could be laid to rest or burned to a cinder and sent down a river. Chelle was far, far away. For now, we were fixed together in the hotel room; we were high on the roof of the world. The country might collapse, the whole world might fall down, but we were safe up here.

I was engaged once. I was married once too, to someone I didn't get engaged to, and I've been divorced once (from the person I had married). I hadn't told Callum that, had I? My ex-husband's name was Frost. I became Lauren Frost for a while, and everyone said I had married him for his name. 'Frost,' they said, 'that suits you.' Of course, I hadn't married him for his name. He also had a good address. He lived in a large house in north London. I didn't get any of it. I didn't want anything from him except the sex. The sex was incredible. He was an earthy type. His fingers were always wandering into places they shouldn't. On our wedding night we were having sex, as you do, and I was on top of him, I think, when suddenly he complained of a terrible headache. I had never heard that excuse used seriously and so I laughed at him. He said, no, really, his head ached; he didn't want to do it again. I don't know if he thought his head might explode or if I hadn't been sympathetic enough or what, but he *really* didn't want to do it again. After six months of celibacy I had, in bewilderment, filed for divorce. My husband looked more relieved than surprised.

'There is no such thing as sex after marriage,' I used to joke to my friends. Now when I think about it, I think, of course there is. There *is* sex after marriage, only it's best if it's with someone else's husband.

I went back to my home town and I found my way back to O'Harts. There was no one there I knew. Everyone had moved on by then. I started a tumultuous affair with a barman who turned out in the end to be Saul the dresser-upper. I didn't know that he was into dressing up for a while, and I think it may have been my fault. We were getting along as happy as Larry when, after about six months, I said, 'Isn't it about time we spice things up? Y'know, in the bedroom?' I didn't really think we should, I think I knew it was over by then, but the magazines said spice was the answer, so I poured it on. Well, Saul was grateful and thankful and overwhelmed with my open-mindedness and, before long, I was back to square one. The single square. All that spice had drowned out the natural flavour.

Sometimes I go too far.

Later Callum and I went out. I felt so proud to be with him. My Callum. But I could feel his tension. He was uneasy being with me in public. He wouldn't even hold my hand.

'I'm not used to this,' he explained.

'What's the worst that can happen? Chelle's down somewhere with the hippos. We're thousands of miles from home. There's no one here we know.'

That was the day I learned what 'famous last words' means.

We decided to do some sightseeing. It's not just Stella and Chelle who can 'do' a city. We watched buses loaded with flowers and we saw a wedding procession go down the street complete with marching band, trumpets and everything. We took off our jackets to enjoy the weak sunshine on the antique steps of an old townhouse and we drank yoghurt drinks in the street while watching some children play hopscotch.

We were both pretty tired by the time we joined the queue to see the famous Stupa that Chelle and Stella had visited that day, all that time ago. Behind us a middle-aged Western couple in Burberry coats and hats were complaining about the unpredictable weather, about the food, about just about everything. I thought they must have been in a different country to us.

I had just that second realised they were staring at us when the woman spoke.

'Callum?'

'Ye-es.' I could hear the hesitation in his voice. He nearly didn't own up to his name.

'What an incredible coincidence! Your mother told us you were honeymooning here but we never thought we would meet up in a million years.'

At first, Callum looked confused rather than horrified.

'I work with your mother. Well, what a small world it really is. Wonderful to meet you too, Chelle, we've heard so much about you. Congratulations.'

'Ah,' I said and, since Callum seemed incapable of forming a sentence, I added, 'and I've heard a lot about you, haven't I, love?'

The silence that spread before us was a great lake in the hot summer. You wanted to strip off and get in it, but it was way too cold.

Callum nodded. I took his hand and gave what I hoped passed as a devoted newly-wed kind of grin.

'We have to rush.' I gripped my stomach and gazed at the ceiling.

'Is it morning sickness, dear? My son was conceived on honeymoon! Callum's mother certainly will be pleased. She's been waiting so long to be a grandmother I think she's almost given up!'

Callum's fingers in my hand were slippery with sweat.

'Oh no, I think it's –' I watched an insect stutter around the light '– malaria.'

'Oh.' The woman sprang back.

'Well, anyway, we have to be off. Bye.'

Callum and I fled from the queue. (So we never did get to see the Stupa after all.)

'Thank fuck,' he said, and he let out a long breath. 'I thought we would never get away from them.'

'Now they are going to tell everyone about meeting you and Chelle. What's going to happen when they meet her?'

'I dunno,' Callum said but, now they had left, he didn't seem particularly worried any more. The worst had happened and we had survived it. 'I'll say you had a boob enlargement or something. Fuck!'

'Fuck indeed!'

'They didn't get it though, did they?' Callum squeezed my hand and didn't let go of it even when we hit the street. We had passed the test. We were home and dry. Well, we were certainly home …

Later, we went back down to the river. We watched people jump in the water, relaxing after work or school. This time, we sat on some steps, under the shadow of some trees and we kissed exuberantly. Even when coach parties stopped right near us, we didn't care. The sadhus stayed away from us too. Then, when it grew colder, Callum let me in his coat and we walked wrapped up in each other and we ate caramelised nuts. It felt so normal and right – like we were a married couple on our honeymoon – that it was ridiculous to think how far from right it was. We watched the sun set over the city, a flaming red ball coming down on to the roof of the world and Callum tightened his hand around my waist.

'Callum,' I whispered, 'I need something hot inside me.'

'More nuts?' He offered me the bag. I pushed it away, laughing.

'Close, but something a bit more substantial is required, I think.'

Callum grinned at me, a great big dirty grin.

'So do you want to go back to the hotel or what?'

We were on the same wavelength, I swear. Sixteen years and we were still tuned in. It wasn't a 'get one over Chelle thing'. It was a him and me thing.

'Nah,' I said, 'it's too far. I can't wait that long.'

'So where then?'

And then I remembered. I couldn't believe that I hadn't thought about it sooner. Hadn't it dominated my dreams? Didn't I sometimes wake in a puddle of sweat, thinking of that woman's face? Didn't I imagine that one day I would meet again the woman with the long shiny hair and the pale-faced man who had kneeled down and licked with such reverence that it was like he was praying?

I said, 'I know a place.'

We walked down the dark corridor. I suppose it was the same as before, but I was more attuned to the tricks the memory plays now; in my imagination, I had made this tunnel bigger and wetter. It was fun watching the place through Callum's eyes though. He behaved like I did when I first went with Stella, full of scepticism, full of jokes. He thought I was crazy, dragging him to this funny old building. What could be here that he hadn't seen a hundred times before?

Just you wait, I thought, you are not going to believe it. Nothing you've ever seen could compare with this. You'll see people fucking each other, you'll see orgies, gangbangs, you name it. Every orientation, every perversion is catered to between and on these walls.

We had arrived. There were only a few people milling around. I hadn't seen a guard yet. I couldn't keep my eyes from the beautifully carved holes in the walls. Did Callum realise yet that, yes, they were life-size holes. Yes, they were what he thought they might be. A couple of men were standing near a particularly attractive-looking slit. I think they were debating whether they could touch it or not. It was funny that you could get attracted to some holes and not others. You could grow really attached.

'Here we are. Is this OK?'

Callum didn't reply. The look on his face, however, told me everything.

We wandered around slowly. He held my hand, he made me wait in front of the things that appealed to him and hurried me past others.

'Here. Stand here.' His voice was hoarse suddenly. Even without looking at him, I would have known he was definitely, indisputably turned on. Even so, it was a shock when he started fondling me. He didn't kiss me but instead pulled up my T-shirt and drank in my bosom lavishly, cramming the whole orb into his mouth, all of it, pulling me on top of him; I had no hope of resisting; my surprise almost overwhelmed my excitement.

Almost, but not completely. He nursed at my bosom, and my nipples were so taut and so upright that they were like steel, pieces of armour.

Callum's strength was back. He was stronger than he ever was. He led me to a chair in the corner of the room. I hadn't seen it last time; odd how I could have missed it, for it wasn't a normal chair; it was covered with images of people fucking. It was, the label next to it said, a 'Kama Sutra chair'. When I sat down it tilted me back and pulled my legs up. I put his hand on my tits again. I wanted to impress him with my boldness and with my willingness. And his face told me he was impressed. Even now, one week in, he was impressed! You know, even a man who *thinks* he likes small tits can't help but be impressed by the large ones.

When we kissed I sighed. Did you know you can sigh even when your mouths are locked around each other, even when your tongues are pressed together, even when there is no place for sound to escape? I pulled away and he smiled at me. He stroked my hair. The sudden tenderness annoyed me. I wanted him to be rough, to get on me right here and now.

I also wanted to see what images appealed to him most.

'Look at the walls,' I said.

'You too,' he said – like I needed the invitation!

I fixed on a scene in the corner. One girl was turned face down. Three or four men were behind her. I looked at another scene. Two girls were rubbing breasts against each other. It was like me and Chelle. Chelle ... why did I think of her? It was like Stella and me, kissing and sucking. There was a man underneath a woman. It was the young porter buckling under the pleasure.

I pulled down my trousers and fingered myself. It was such a relief to feel something in there. What was

Callum looking at? He was looking at me. Callum breathed into my ear.

'You're so hot. Look at you. You just can't help yourself. I just want to . . .'

'Please do.' I found the scene of the woman tied down and the monks. I knew exactly what that was like. Oh Christ, and I knew exactly why she looked like that. It was me. It was me. I was sure of it. They had held me down and they had secured me on to the table like that. It was the same table with the wide ornate legs and there was nothing else in the room. There were close-ups of fingers going in and out and thighs spread wider and her face, the ecstasy of her face as the punishment reached its culmination.

'Oh God . . .'

As soon as Callum climbed on top of me I knew I wouldn't last a second. I think he said, 'I'm going to watch you come,' but he might have said 'we' because I knew we weren't alone in the room, but I was up there in Nirvana. Up there with the moon, the stars; the universe was too small to contain a passion like ours. My eyes opened just for a second to see a flash of an orgy scene; there were arses and tits in my eye, everything was fucking me. I let my eyelids drop as the pleasure washed over and over me. When I opened my eyes again, all I could see were two Burberry mackintoshes and faces distorted into Picasso paintings of anger. But it was too late by then, I was coming, and I couldn't stop screaming and shaking and smashing my arms against his back for more.

'Oh yes. Oh yes. Oh God, I'm sorry!'

'I can't believe what we did.' In the coffee shop, Callum was full of remorse. 'And they saw us too. My parents' friends actually saw us fucking!'

'Well they shouldn't have been there,' I said flatly.

'I must be the biggest shit in the world,' Callum said glumly. He added more sugar to his coffee and stirred it vigorously. It was his second cup.

'You've got a conscience, that's good.' I was starving but it didn't seem appropriate to eat. Now I just picked at the sides of the small chocolate cake I had ordered.

'Like having a conscience means anything!'

It's more than your fucking wife has! I thought. I wouldn't have liked Callum if he didn't care. He wouldn't have been my man. I knew that I shouldn't have been doing this either. Where was my sense of feminine solidarity? And if not that, where was my common sense? This wasn't going anywhere. And yet, and yet this wasn't about common sense or Chelle. It wasn't about a future; it was about now. It was about now or the next few seconds until we could get together again. It was about longing for his mouth to ride on mine again.

'What's the point?' he said. He put his teaspoon down on the serviette and we watched it stain the white triangle brown. 'What's the fucking point of anything?'

I remember Callum's end of term art show. I think this was only about two weeks before we split, so I suppose Rose was already racing around in my bloodstream although I hadn't admitted it even to myself. I really wanted to see the art on show, in an exhibition; wouldn't that be what we had been working towards? But there was some kind of administrative mix-up and Callum only had two tickets. He knew he wanted me to go. It was most important that I be there; I was the most important person in his world, right? But we both knew that if I went it meant either his mum or dad couldn't go. We argued, in our cuddling, hugging way, but it did go on for quite a while. Finally, I convinced him that his parents should go. Not me. I would wait outside.

Outside, a tall girl with bright red hair came over to me. She was waiting for her friend too, she explained. She was just chatting about this and that when suddenly her manner changed completely.

'Are you Callum's girlfriend?'

'Ye-es,' I said. I was nervous of Callum's art school friends. They all seemed so sophisticated, so self-assured.

'Wow. He talks about you all the time. You're just as he said.'

'Oh . . .'

'You are so lucky. Callum is absolutely head over heels about you,' she said, and she swayed a little and I realised for all her sophistication and self-assurance that she was a little in love with him too.

'Aren't I?'

Then I saw Callum and his mum and dad coming out of the swing doors to see me. The pride on their faces was something else. Callum got to me before they did.

'Thank you,' he said as he kissed me. 'I really appreciate what you did.'

Aren't I lucky?

After we got back to the hostel that evening, I tried to reason with him.

'It's not that bad, Cal. A lot of people have –' I didn't know what word to use to describe us '– relationships outside marriage.'

'I never thought I would be one of them.'

He was so down on himself and yet all I could think was that, yes, here the real Callum was seeping out. He used to be like this, not for long of course, but sometimes, and I was glad he was sharing his thoughts with me. I was sure I could talk him round.

'How many people did you sleep with before you married Chelle?'

I had him down for about seven or eight. He wasn't the promiscuous sort, for sure.

'I dunno,' he muttered. Callum clearly didn't want to talk about it. Maybe he was embarrassed that the number would be lower than mine was. Men hate that.

'Just approximately?' I pushed.

'About a hundred, I suppose, I really don't know.'

'Oh,' I said, losing track of where I was taking this conversation. Callum had been inside about a hundred women. What was with the 'about'? Couldn't he be more accurate? Had he come inside all of them? Did he really shoot off in one hundred different pussies or did he just mean that he had kissed a hundred girls. Yes, that had to be it.

'You mean snogging, right?'

'No, I mean sex. That's what you asked.'

'Oh.' I decided this was one issue I had to let go. 'Anyway, the point is ... Is it really sleeping with someone else if you sleep with me?'

'Eh?'

'It's not like the number of women you slept with would change, is it? You've already slept with me once. It kind of makes no difference if you do it again.'

'So I could sleep with any of those hundred women again and it wouldn't be being unfaithful to Chelle?'

That wasn't exactly what I meant. The thought of Callum sleeping with any of those hundred women was worse than the thought of him sleeping with Chelle. At least he was semi-obligated to sleep with Chelle.

'No, I mean, if you slept with me, Callum, that it wouldn't mean you were being unfaithful. It would be like being in a time warp, like going back in time and finishing the job, as it were. How else can I put it?'

'Like closure?'

'I don't see why it has to be closure though. It's just ... just going back in time. Like every year, we put the clocks back. This would just be the ... the sexual equivalent of that. When you put the clocks back, you don't feel like you're being unfaithful to the seasons do you? You just feel it's the right thing to do, yeah?'

'So sleeping with you is the right thing to do now?'

'Not necessarily,' I said quickly. 'But it's not necessarily the wrong thing to do either.'

Callum rubbed his eyes. He looked very weary. I kept forgetting how ill he had been. He pulled at my hand and kissed it. The smile he gave me was rueful.

'The problem is not that I slept with you, but that I want to fuck you again and again and again. And I can't see that ever ending ... I mean, each time I do it, I don't want it to end. Each time it ends, I want to do it again, well, after a sleep of course.' He smiled wryly. 'Each time I wake up, I want to see you. I want to go to bed at night with you. I want you to know everything about me. I can't imagine ever wanting to be with anyone else again ... and that includes my wife.'

Callum had bought expensive tickets for a song and dance 'extravaganza' at one of the few Western hotels in the city. It was another of the Kathmandu-must-dos. There was a five-course meal and a firework display too. We began walking there. He thought it would only take about twenty minutes, but on the way we changed our minds, and not because it was too far. We walked the whole way back to the hostel silently. Once the decision was made not to go, we didn't speak at all, and once the bedroom door was shut behind us, we fell on each other. I knew instinctively that Callum had decided this was our last time and I had to make it last. He gripped my hair with a passion I had never seen in him. He pinned me down on the bed like I was a criminal, a thief in the night. I suppose I was in a way.

He said, 'No more arguments. No more games.'

'OK.'

'OK then.'

We were kissing the faces off each other. We were sucking the lips out of each other, and all the time we were watching each other. Our eyes were wide open. I was staring, drowning in his pupils. I was watching the arch of his eyelid, the curve of his brow as he ate my lips. I didn't let up against him for a second.

This time, when I felt him come close, and I was coming close, it was like we were both drawing towards the same thing, and I needn't have worried about separate speeds or anything like that; we marched forwards towards it together. He gave me a sign and his fucking became faster and faster, clockwork soldier on speed, and he rammed home, and we were both there together, together, forever.

So we waited for Chelle and Stella separately. That was what Callum wanted, although he did protest, 'It's not what I *want*, Lauren. It's just the way things have to be.'

Is there a difference? I have to admit we did once have an argument before we parted. I was telling him Nepalese theories about re-incarnation and about my own theories on the subject. Callum brushed my cheek.

'So, baby, what were you in a past life?' he asked.

'A prostitute,' I smirked. 'A wild sexy whore.'

'I said in a past life!' he laughed.

Well, I didn't find that very funny and I told him as much.

The next morning, I took the room Stella and I had taken before at The Everest and Callum left Les Trois Peaks and took his old room across the town. I couldn't open the bedroom window and I had to get the receptionist to help unstick it. When he came up, he looked around the room shyly and said, 'Now the English lady becomes a nun, hey, hey!'

'You're not Benny Hill,' I said.

'Benny Hill?' he said. 'Ha ha! He is very funny!'

With the window open, I breathed in the city air and heard the cry of the taxis and the swish of the women walking in their saris. I waited for him. I was still sure that Callum and I would be together again soon. What I didn't know was how.

I was living a thousand what-ifs:

What if Chelle came back and knew? What if she threw him out and he blamed me? What if he couldn't look at me because the sight of me made him so angry?

What if Chelle came back and she knew? What if she threw him out and he came to me?

What if Chelle came back and she didn't know? What if he told her and then he came to me?

What if Chelle came back and she didn't know? What if he didn't tell her and they went back to their little life in Stonebridge Wells or wherever it was, and no one ever found out?

One afternoon, I took a bus to the zoo. I went on my own although one of the receptionists said they had a brother who would love to take me. Nudge, nudge. I said no, thank you. I didn't think I would ever go on a date again although as it turned out it probably would have been good to have some company. For a country with so much wildlife, Kathmandu zoo was a disappointment. But then I realised that it was because you couldn't keep those animals cooped up. You couldn't capture something as beautiful and as wild and as free as they were. That is, you could try to capture them. You could dress them up, label them and put them in an institution, but it probably wouldn't work.

The days were miserable but the nights and the mornings had to be worse. In the afternoon I wandered around the city like I was in a dream. Only small children and street-traders spoke to me. 'Hello, lady, do you want to buy something?' I ate alone in cafés, quickly and always with a newspaper in front of me. But in the afternoons, I knew Callum was still somewhere, still out in the city. I could smell him. He was nearby, I knew it. I was so sure I would bump into him that I never left the hostel until I was dressed perfectly. People always find each other in films. But although I saw plenty of people who looked like him – was Nepal filled with Callum look-a-likes that week? – I never saw him. Perhaps, I consoled myself, he was watching me?

In the night, I had no such illusions. In the night, I couldn't even pretend he was with me because his absence was so huge. In the morning when, half in sleep, I rolled joyfully towards the middle of the bed, towards the warmth radiating from him, it was agony to rediscover that he wasn't there.

Eventually Stella came back. She came the same time, I suppose, as Chelle went back to him. I heard her thundering along the hostel corridor and I rushed out to greet her. Tears of relief prickled my eyes. Stella hugged me tight and then she threw herself on the bed and you could just tell she was bursting to tell me something although, politely, she was going to wait until I asked.

'What happened, Stella?' I asked quickly because when we talked about her at least we weren't talking about Callum and me. I remember that is a way to deal with naughty kids. You don't try to reason with them – they have no reason – your only tool is distraction. It's the only thing that works on two-year-olds and lovesick thirty-two-year-olds.

'You'll never guess what happened!' she said.

'You and Chelle had a good ol' gang-bang on top of Mount Everest? You're in the record books as the first lesbian couple to do it up there.'

That made Stella a little annoyed. She did her why-are-you-behaving-like-this face. 'No, nothing like that.'

It was Raj. Apparently, the guide who wasn't a guide confessed all to Stella and, to apologise for his deceit, he took her to his village home and they had a huge party and...'

'Hold on,' I said. 'Where was Chelle all this time?'

'She was in Chitwan,' Stella said awkwardly. 'She met someone. A woman.' She added, unnecessarily I think, 'You would have hated her.'

Weren't Stella and Callum good enough for Chelle? Good God, she would stop at no one. She reminded me of someone but I couldn't work out whom.

'Anyway, Raj took me back to this room. I had this weird feeling that there was someone else there, but it didn't really bother me, until Raj blindfolded me.'

'He what?'

'He blindfolded me and I know, I know, I shouldn't have let him, under the circumstances, but he said it was an ancient Nepali custom.'

'An ancient custom?'

'It was amazing.'

'Well, go on . . .'

'Raj took off my clothes. I knew it was him. You get used to someone. Someone's hands I mean. Everyone's feel different even when they try to be the same; perhaps especially when they try to be the same. Besides, I could smell Raj. Do you remember the way he smelled?'

I nodded, even though I didn't. I suppose I was too busy sniffing around the others.

'But then I'm sure the other person came over to me and he started stroking me as well. It wasn't said. Raj didn't say, here is my friend, but I could just tell that someone else was joining in.'

'And?'

'Well, it was a most peculiar feeling. I felt really secure, legitimised. I could do anything that I liked and it was all right, almost holy even because it was all . . .'

'Part of an ancient Nepali custom?'

'Exactly.'

'The thing was, I couldn't stop thinking of the temple. And there was this image there – I don't know if you saw it. You said once that you had. It was of a woman surrounded by these men and surrendering herself to them, or not to them really, but to the pleasure they were giving her. And when I thought of that, I couldn't help myself. I would have done anything they wanted while that was in my mind.'

'So did they?'

'Oh yes,' she said cheerily. 'Once they realised that I wasn't going to object, far from it, I had them both, at the same time. Double penetration, I think it's called. I didn't ever want it to end.'

'It sounds amazing,' I said finally. I didn't know if I was jealous or not. 'Only I can't believe you were taken in by all that part of an ancient Nepali custom bullshit.'

'Don't you understand?' she said shyly. 'I wanted to be taken in.'

I suppose that was how Callum had felt too. He knew it was madness to be with me but, for a while, he wanted to believe it was OK. So he allowed the deceit to continue. It made me think there must be a lot of this self-deceit stuff about.

I don't know when it started but Stella's hands were whispering between my legs and, I have to confess, it *was* making me feel better. I hadn't thought anything would, but this did. I tentatively put my fingers to her place and that wasn't bad at all either. She was the same as me, but she wasn't. And that wetness, the gushing from her slit, made me feel like I really was good at this. I had found my forte. Forget the best wet T-shirt in Kathmandu, I was the best lover in the whole world. Wow, I could really turn her on. Even if for some reason she suddenly announced that she didn't like it, well, I knew better – the proof was in her pussy!

So we sat there comforting each other in our white sticky feminine wetness, our long hot wet women's kisses. Then Stella came down and was sucking my tits. It was weird but, when I say that, I don't mean that it was weird in a negative way, not at all. I don't think she expected me to reciprocate until suddenly she pulled away, and I thought, shit, I've really annoyed her. She got up and marched over to her rucksack. I thought she was going to tell me I was lazy or a prude or something but, instead, she took out a box and I realised she wasn't angry with me. This was about something else.

'Chelle asked me to look after this. It's a souvenir of her honeymoon.'

She took out a Tibetan singing bell with a ringer. The ringer was about hand size, a nice wood carved into a slim cucumber shape. The bell was copper I think, with a fat base and a thin ornamental top. It was unremark-able until Stella started to rub the ringer around the base of the bell. The sound that carried was a pure note that, as she rubbed more and more, grew louder and louder, until I thought it would break mirrors or glass or windows. I mean, it really had an incredible power.

'That's cool,' I said. I wanted Stella's lips back. I wanted her pussy again. I could really get to like that. Finger-fucking. I thought back briefly to the monk who touched me while I cleaned the bath; hmm, it was even better when it was a two-way thing. But I was also feeling a little concerned. Stella, darling, I wanted to know, but I didn't dare ask, why are you playing this now? Don't you like me any more?

Then Stella said, 'Well, I wonder what on earth we can do with it?' She fingered the ringer thoughtfully.

'Eh? Oh, yes, right, OK. This is Chelle's, you say?'

'Uh huh. I have to give it back to her soon but until then, it's all ours.'

Stella tilted me backwards and very delicately, in the way only she could, she spread my thighs. She pressed her fingers up my hole tenderly and held me open wide. The moment before the ringer went inside was incred-ible. The anticipation was overwhelming. Then I felt the wooden stick move up me and I had to hold my breath. Brilliant. Why didn't I think of that? Whenever Chelle rang that bell and thought of her honeymoon in Nepal, how sweet it was to know that it would always smell of me.

Stella said Chelle had told her about a hostel across the city that had an outdoor pool. The next morning, Stella asked if I wanted to come, but she was a little doubtful as though she hoped I would say no. It was like when she asked if I wanted to go trekking with them.

'Of course,' I said, as Stella had feared. I would do anything to be close to them. Anything to see Callum suffer the way I was suffering.

So we went to the pool.

They were playing volleyball. They were swiping it over the net next to the pool. Chelle bounded around. She was hefty and strong. Her shoulders trembled each time she hit the ball. Her bikini top barely managed to contain her breasts. It was red and white stripes. She had boobs that looked too far apart. The bikini bottoms were a little too big and she kept hoisting them up. You could see she liked having to do that, she liked the way it said, 'I've lost weight.' Her hair was wet and she kept pushing it back even though it wasn't getting in her eyes. She did have pretty eyes, I suppose.

Suddenly I thought of Dave. That's who she reminded me of.

Callum was still looking a bit thin around the middle but he looked fitter than he had done in a long time. He reminded me a bit of the boy he used to be. He was wearing black swimming trunks; I think they were new; I hadn't seen them before. Another one of Chelle's honeymoon souvenirs probably. He was jumping around a lot; he must have fully recovered. This environment suited him of course. Better than some mountain trail. What did someone like him care about mountains?

He dived into the pool first. He went down, down, down and just when I felt the panic rise inside me, he popped up, far from where he had disappeared and he was laughing. Callum was happy again. He swam long cool strokes to the side, disturbing the beautiful smoothness of that blue water with something even more beautiful.

'Come on, baby, are you coming in?'

Chelle walked down the steps, complaining of the cold. She shivered. I couldn't see the goose pimples on her arms, around her breasts, but I'm sure they were there. Finally, she reached him; they cuddled and kissed. I think he played with her breasts under the water. He circled around her and then he stood against her, his head pressed into her shoulder. Her arm wrapped around him, locking him there, the way a policeman might trap a criminal.

And then he looked up, over to where I was standing. I know that he saw me. He didn't wave.

16

'Do you love him then?'

Chelle was standing at the end of my bed in a white T-shirt and tiny denim shorts – they were like the shorts I used to wear. She knew he liked them I suppose.

'Of course not,' I lied. I wasn't that surprised that she was there.

'He's changed.'

'It has nothing to do with me.'

'It had better not have.'

She took off her T-shirt and her shorts. She wasn't wearing anything underneath as I had guessed. I arched my legs up and she moved to sit by me on the bed. I was naked. Chelle didn't say anything else, but she put her hand on my leg. When I asked her what she was doing, what the hell she thought she was doing, she answered by inserting her fingers inside me. Her fingers were massaging my cunt. I pulled them away, once, twice, but then I let her; I almost meowed with the pleasure. I couldn't believe this. I lay on my back and let her play with me. If that's what she wanted to do then who was I to stop her? In bed, she was as she was in real life: brusque and wildly efficient. I thrust up to her, pushing my cunt against her. I could be as vicious as she was.

'Hold your legs apart, Lauren, wider. I want to get in there.'

'Oh yes, more,'

She pulled my pussy lips apart and slipped her tongue around me.

'You like that?'

'I love it.'

'Now you. I want you to lick my pussy. Turn yourself around.'

She shifted and this time we were in 69 and I had the first shock of her cunt over my face. Our heads were between each other's legs. I must have been concentrating really hard because I didn't know how exactly I had got there. All I knew was that it was really something to have luscious hair pressing against your thighs; your face mashed against warm, milky cunt.

'You want that?'

'Oh please.'

We were both of us in time with each other, mirroring each other's noises, mirroring each other's bodies.

'Now I understand why Callum liked you!' I said to her muff. Christ, it was hot down there. I hadn't realised.

'Ditto! Lick me more please, Lauren. Lick me.'

'Oh God!'

'Keep up, Lauren!' she ordered, but I realised I quite liked it. I found myself desperate to please her. I would do anything to make her happy.

'And your finger,' she demanded, for even now, even with me lapping at her like a fucking lunatic, even now she wasn't satisfied. Was she ever the bossy cow?

'Put a finger up me. I can't come unless you put your finger up my arsehole.'

'Umm, it's not something I . . .'

But resistance to Chelle was futile. I should have known I would end up out of my depth.

'Here.' She pulled my finger in her mouth and sucked on it like it were a cock. 'Do it.'

Her mouth was warm and wet.

'Usually . . . I don't . . .'

'OK, now, here.'

She pulled my hand to her arse. My finger slid inside her and her buttocks quivered and shrank around me, and then I was overcome by the weirdness of it all and the unexpectedness. I licked and licked her pussy. This wasn't so difficult; it was as natural as the air and the mountains and she was as red as a flame and on fire and on top of me, and I rubbed and we rubbed our bodies. As she came, she sucked tight at my pussy. She was fierce and violent and my clit ached in her mouth.

When I woke from the dream (or was it a night-mare?) the sheet was wet with my juices and I had to masturbate. I got the wooden stick of her ringing bell and cried as I rubbed it up and down, reliving the images. What the hell was going on here?

Stella was right. This place did get to you. And the demons, they were still there, chasing after me.

Repeat after me. Callum is a weak useless man. He married Chelle, for goodness' sake, a bossy, domineering bitch. He used to shoplift just to please me. What kind of idiot thinks he can do that? He didn't even shoplift on his own but with someone else! He never resisted it when I finished with him; he never fought to be with me. He didn't move mountains to be with me. He works in insurance when he doesn't really want to. He has the talent of an artist but he wastes it on accounts. He deceived me into thinking he was innocent of what I was doing. He is an adulterer – it's an old-fashioned word but it's true. He has a conscience but does not act on it. He has no power of his convictions. He is every-thing that is mundane. I need someone strong; I need someone who wouldn't tie the knot just because it was 'the thing to do'. I want someone who wouldn't put up with a girl like Chelle. I want someone of my own. I know all this; yet still it makes no difference; I love him.

We were at a table in the garden of a restaurant towards the north of the city. It was like the first time, the first night we were all together, but now I didn't even have hope. And we were one extra. Raj had come along. He followed Stella everywhere now.

Chelle was exuberant, radiant from her adventures. The 'other' woman is the one who is supposed to be more attractive, or younger, or more bubbly, or at least more something than the wronged wife, but I wasn't any of them. I was pallid; I felt despondent. As for Callum, I noticed now I was only a foot away from him, his eyes were red from lack of sleep. His skin, so pale since his illness, was tinged green.

When we arrived, he looked up at me, and I could see etched on his features was one question: why did you have to come?

I wished I hadn't.

How Chelle and Stella could talk! How the mountains were incredible! How it was totally different from whatever you had heard. No, really, *you had to be there*.

'We *were* there,' Callum said wearily, like he had heard this a thousand times a day.

'No,' Chelle insisted. 'You weren't there all the time and it was really *different* at the top.'

I didn't dare look at Callum because I was thinking, it is the same with love. You couldn't imagine how it felt like until it hit you, smack bang in the solar plexus. And then you got what all the fuss was about. Especially unrequited love. Yes, especially that.

I noticed that each time the conversation got on to

something potentially 'awkward', Stella would discreetly guide it into a less uncomfortable direction. If Chelle went on about being a wife, Stella would talk about work. If Chelle started on sex, Stella would butt in with a joke.

Stella was great.

The waiter came to take our orders. Callum couldn't decide between the buffalo or the chicken. The waiter didn't care. He smiled then shrugged. 'You have all the time in the world.'

But we didn't. They were leaving the next day. Callum and Chelle were flying back to England. The honeymoon was over.

Chelle told Callum to have chicken.

'Your stomach is still weak,' she insisted, like he was a child. 'Buffalo meat is far too tough for you. Have something that you know you like.'

I should have argued but I couldn't.

'I don't know,' Callum said. 'It's my last night.'

He said it like it was his last night before his execution.

Chelle laughed, nodding at Stella. 'I told you, he's so fucking indecisive. If he didn't have me to take care of him, I don't know what he would do.'

Stella interrupted to tell us that some countries were developing chickens without feathers.

'God,' said Chelle, 'what will they think of next? Developing fannies without pubic hair?'

I watched as Chelle passed around her photos. I realised I was jealous of her and, actually, it wasn't just because of Callum. In the week they had spent together, Chelle and Stella seemed to have become even firmer friends than ever. I don't think it would be true now if Stella said she preferred me to Chelle.

'Some honeymoon, we haven't had sex for three weeks!' Chelle moaned.

Even Stella couldn't talk out of that one.

Once, five years ago, our paths almost crossed. I had gone to stay with my parents for a couple of days. It was just after my wedding and I was just trying to work out why Mr Frost didn't want sex with me. One night, I called up a friend who still lived in town and she arranged to meet me at what was O'Harts and which was now part of a high-street pub chain with huge glass windows, chrome tables and staff who wore uniforms that matched the décor of the loos. (Saul would have enjoyed that.) For some reason, I can't even remember why now, I ended up getting there half an hour late. My friend scolded me; she had arranged a baby-sitter, for goodness' sake, time was money, and didn't I realise how embarrassing it was for her to be waiting on her own in a bar like Bessy No-mates?

It wasn't until I had bought her a couple of doubles that she thought to tell me, 'You'll never guess who was here earlier . . . someone I haven't seen for ages.'

When she told me it was Callum, I just said, 'Oh yeah?' and we started talking about local nurseries or something like that. I found I couldn't speak about him at all. So all the questions I had – What did he look like? What was he wearing? Who was he with? – stayed unasked.

Sometimes I wonder what would have happened if I had been there on time.

Raj left the table to chat with some friends who were drinking at the other side of the garden. I suppose some of them were quite good looking but I wasn't interested.

I *had* Callum and, like the mountains here, he made everything else insignificant in comparison.

Stella needed the loo. Chelle said that she would go with her. The waiter said the closest one was a way down the street.

It was me who asked how long it would take to get there.

'Five minutes,' the waiter said, 'if you hurry.'

With any luck there would be a queue. Callum and I might be alone for over ten minutes. With any luck there would be a coachload of Germans wrapped in ski gear, unable to find their zips. Callum and I would have a whole ten minutes, at least.

I almost admired Chelle for her innocence, or was it her confidence? If I were her, I wouldn't have left Callum alone with me.

Please let there be Germans there. Or Italians. Actually anyone would do. As long as there was a busload of people there I would be happy.

As they left, Chelle said, 'Lauren, you won't believe some of the loos I've seen up those mountains.'

I raised my eyebrows in a way that I hoped was encouraging although I was wondering why the hell she thought I would be interested.

'I'll tell you when I get back.'

'Great. Wonderful. I look forward to that.'

Then Chelle came at Callum as though she had forgotten something and gave him this big fishlike kiss on the lips.

'Honey, we'll have our *proper* honeymoon later.'

It was all for my benefit.

As soon as they were out the gate, probably before they were out of it actually, Callum whispered, 'Come here, sit next to me.'

I walked around the table to him. It didn't cross my mind to say no.

We faced the restaurant, but no one was taking any notice of us. I didn't know what he was going to do. I thought he might say, 'It should never have happened,' or 'Forgive me,' or something stoical.

He didn't say anything. Instead his hand landed on my breast and he started kissing me. His mouth was on mine, pressed on mine, and his tongue was in my mouth, where it should be. Where it had to be. He swirled and darted there and I did the same thing to him. I wanted to keep my eyes open, but they closed – a reflex. My tits were aching for him. I pushed him back once, but I didn't mean it, and he knew I didn't.

'We shouldn't. This is madness,' I managed to say. 'How can we go on?'

'How can we stop?'

We had ten little minutes. My nipples were like bullets between his fingers, hard stones. He gripped them tight, pulling at them. I responded not only there, but deeper down in my lower body. I was wet between the legs.

Please touch me there too, Callum.

'I want you now, Lauren.'

We had ten minutes, less now. I couldn't stop.

'Yes,' I whispered. There was nothing else I could say to convey how much I wanted him.

'Oh God, let me touch you. I want you. You're so horny.'

Who said that he was indecisive?

I was wearing the dress I had worn that first day as we walked by the river. Perhaps as I put it on earlier that evening I had guessed this might happen. Perhaps, subconsciously, I had hoped. Still, while it was happening, I couldn't believe that it was. Callum slid his hand up my thigh. First he felt one and then the other, and then his fingers were rubbing both thighs, at the top. No one nearby was any the wiser. (This was so much better than struggling with a trouser zip.)

I was almost embarrassed at how wet my knickers were. He might think I had peed myself for God's sake. He pulled his mouth from mine and whispered between my lips, 'You know you want it.'

Then Callum was pinching at the side of my knickers, I mean the underneath bit, the bit between my legs, and each little exposure made me sigh and stuff my tongue in his mouth more madly. I don't know why I wanted to do that, I just did. I wanted to get my tongue in there, right in there, gobble him up. Callum pulled back the knickers but he didn't put his fingers inside me. I was open wide but he didn't enter me straight away. Instead his fingers just hovered there, teasing me around my entrance. He must have known I was melting. I forgot the time, forgot everything. In my head I was screaming for him to get in there, please touch me.

Callum was still kissing me, firmer, harder. He was saying that I mustn't resist. He was saying that with his tongue holding me in place.

We had seven, eight minutes at the most. We were in a public place. How much further could we go? His fingers moved. Almost. Nearly. Yes. He pressed himself against my cunt. They were up me, at long fucking last. The way I wanted them. His shorts were bulging. He couldn't keep himself down. I couldn't decide: could we fuck or not? Could we go all the way here?

'We have to stop,' I lied, and then I French kissed him so madly, so deeply, that I thought he might get annoyed.

And then a few seconds later I said, 'Hey, hey, enough . . .'

But then we were kissing again, and teasing and his fingers were playing with my clit and everything and I knew I couldn't stop. I was fit to explode. But I knew his fingers, glorious as they were, weren't enough. Not now. Not for the last time. For the final time – if this is what it was going to be – I needed his cock.

'One for the road?' he asked, only it wasn't a question.

Callum pulled me on top of him so that I straddled him, like he was a horse. I felt his cock poking and prodding at me, and all I had to do was hold it down and slide into place, and there was a moment there when I could have said no, but there wasn't a moment at all. I moved over him, I guided him in until I was full of him. I was riding him, and as he slid his cock up me, I thought, Oh Christ, someone might see, but then his dick filled me up and there was no going back.

'Lauren, you are fantastic. Oh God, you are the best.'

He licked over my ear. It made the hairs on my arm stand on end.

'I want you. You are so horny. There's no one like you. You're the best. I can't live without you. I must have you, always, now, always. I'm going to make you come, like you've never fucking come in your life. I need you. I'll do anything for you and your hot cunt.'

He was all over me and I was wrapped over him. And I didn't believe his words, not for a moment, but I loved them.

'Come for me, baby. Show me how you come.'

I moved up and down but I was subtle, like a beginner. I was just doing short stroking movements up and down his shaft. Yes, like that. I didn't want anyone to see but I knew I couldn't do it like this for long. He had to go deeper. Please.

'I want to see you come.'

I had to go for more. I had to really grind up and down on his cock, the real in and out kind of fucking. I couldn't help it. I've heard people say that sex is like a runaway train, and that's how I was then; coming at him, up and down, no brakes, no end in sight; all Callum could do was sit back and enjoy the ride. And he was enjoying it. He fiddled with my nipples, drooling, as I fucked him, up and down, in and out. I never dreamed we would be able to do it again.

Or that we would do it so publicly.

We had been noticed. The garden wall behind us was only about a metre high and it backed on to a street leading to some of the city's older hostels. Footsteps stopped. I pretended I didn't know, but we were being watched.

I hoped Callum didn't realise for he would have made us stop, but I knew and I couldn't help myself.

They were tourists. Australians, I think, but I didn't care who or what they were, as long as nothing got between me and my Callum.

Up and down, up and down. I was trekking up the mountain of his cock. And we were building up into that momentum that only people who are right for each other can do when he took me by surprise. With the hand that wasn't tweaking my nipples, he was cupping my buttocks, under my skirt of course. Then he moved his hand around and sank his fingers into my arsehole. I suppose he wanted to speed up things and it certainly had the desired effect for I turned into a mad thing, smashing up and down on him, flapping and writhing, my tits soaring over him.

He might not have seen the spectators, but he must have heard the shouting all right. They were yelling: 'You go, girl,' and 'Give it to him!'

I couldn't stop. I couldn't stop. All I could do was

push him away, so the friction was harder, so that I was nearly there.

'She's pretending.'

I heard one of the other men say, 'Fuck, man, she's not acting. She's really going for it.'

'If she is faking it, she deserves an Oscar.'

I could feel their stares on my tits, on my arse. Oh yes, an Oscar, stick it up me. Stick everything up me. I deserved this. I had been a good girl. I could feel their admiration as I worked Callum and when he slathered his tongue all over my tits – he really isn't indecisive, Chelle – my anus clenched, my clit clenched and my pussy too. I wasn't aware of anything except for this incredible, unstoppable grinding unison; him and me, me and him. He came inside me in one, two, three great convulsions.

There was a big round of applause. If I hadn't been pretending that I didn't know they were there, I would have turned and bowed. Instead I buried my head in Callum's shoulder and when I had caught my breath enough to speak, I whispered, 'Do you think anyone noticed?'

By the time Chelle and Stella came back, we were both sipping cold beer. My arse was sore where he plundered so violently. His come was inside me. Callum's come was inside me. And part of me, that part of me, was thinking, so fuck you, Chelle.

After the waiter delivered a pancake and five plates, a blind man and his friend stood at our table. I thought they wanted food so I offered a spoon but Chelle snatched it back. 'You don't know where he's been.'

The blind man didn't want the food anyway. He stood there, not watching us but surveying us somehow. Then he spoke to his friend and the friend translated.

'I see you are in love,' he said.

Raj said something in Nepali quickly, but the pair would not be silenced. I didn't know what he was saying but I sensed that Raj was anxious that they go away soon. He picked his nose and smoothed back his hair.

'Big, big, powerful love.'

Chelle preened. She tossed back her hair and grasped Callum's hand.

'I smell sex.'

The blind man's friend pushed my and Callum's heads together. Raj bent down as if to do up a shoelace, only I knew he didn't have shoes with laces; he didn't even wear shoes. He was hiding his face because he was so embarrassed. Stella was biting her lip so hard that it turned first white and then blue, but Chelle, Chelle still hadn't got it; Chelle was rigorously dividing the dessert into five portions so that we all would have, according to her, an equal share.

'Your love is too big for this life but next life you will be forever together.'

Callum got up. He took out some money, crumpled notes with the King of Nepal's head on them, and left them on the table. He didn't speak, not a word. I remember seeing someone after they had witnessed an accident, and I think he was like that, he was in shock. He moved automatically. I don't think he was aware of any of us.

As he walked away, I knew that, this time, I wouldn't see him again.

Stella said why didn't we have a nightcap? She had heard they did a great coffee here. No one answered her. Chelle faffed around for so long with her purse and her jacket that I thought she would never leave. She wouldn't meet my eye, but I didn't try to meet hers. I had wanted her to find out, but not like this.

And then I realised she knew. I should have known; she probably knew all along. She wasn't stupid. She had just been pretending. We all had been pretending. She was just about to go when she turned to me. I think it was a spur of the moment thing; that is, I don't think she could have planned it, but you never know.

She said, 'Well, Lauren, I still haven't thanked you properly for bringing Callum down.'

Visit the Black Lace website at
www.blacklace-books.co.uk

FIND OUT THE LATEST INFORMATION AND TAKE ADVANTAGE OF OUR FANTASTIC FREE BOOK OFFER! ALSO VISIT THE SITE FOR . . .

- All Black Lace titles currently available and how to order online
- Great new offers
- Writers' guidelines
- Author interviews
- An erotica newsletter
- Features
- Cool links

BLACK LACE – THE LEADING IMPRINT OF WOMEN'S SEXY FICTION

TAKING YOUR EROTIC READING PLEASURE TO NEW HORIZONS

LOOK OUT FOR THE ALL-NEW BLACK LACE BOOKS – AVAILABLE NOW!

All books priced £6.99 in the UK. Please note publication dates apply to the UK only. For other territories, please contact your retailer.

WICKED WORDS 9
Various
ISBN 0352 33860 1

Wicked Words collections are the hottest anthologies of women's erotic writing to be found anywhere in the world. With settings and scenarios to suit all tastes, this is fun erotica at the cutting edge from the UK and USA. The diversity of themes and styles reflects the multi-faceted nature of the female sexual imagination. Combining humour, warmth and attitude with imaginative writing, these stories sizzle with horny action. **Another scorching collection of wild fantasies.**

FEMININE WILES
Karina Moore
ISBN 0 352 33874 1

Young American art student Kelly Aslett is spending the summer in Paris before flying back to California to claim her inheritance when she falls in lust and love with gorgeous French painter, Luc Duras. But her stepmother – the scheming and hedonistic Marissa – is determined to claim the luxury house for herself. Still in love with Luc, Kelly is horrified to find herself sexually entranced by the enigmatic figure of Johnny Casigelli, a ruthless but very sexy villain Marissa has enlisted in her scheme to wrestle the inheritance away from Kelly. Will she succumb to his masculine charms, or can she use her feminine wiles to gain what is rightfully hers? **A high-octane tale of erotic obsession and sexual rivalry.**

Coming in March

GOING DEEP
Kimberley Dean
ISBN 0 352 33876 8

Sporty Brynn Montgomery returns to teach at the college where she used to be a cheerleader but, to her horror, finds that football player Cody Jones, who scandalised her name ten years previously, is now the coach. Soon Brynn is caught up in a clash of pads, a shimmer of pom-poms and the lust of healthy athletes. However, Cody is still a wolfish predator and neither he nor his buddies are going to let Brynn forget what she did that fateful night back in high school. **Rip-roaring, testosterone-fuelled fun set among the jocks and babes of the Ivy League.**

UNHALLOWED RITES
Martine Marquand
ISBN 0 352 33222 0

Twenty-year-old Allegra is bored with life in her guardian's Venetian palazzo – until temptation draws her to look at the curious pictures he keeps in his private chamber. Physically awakened to womanhood, she tries to deny her new passion by submitting to life as a nun. But the strange order of the Convent of Santa Clesira provides new tests and temptations, forcing her to perform ritual acts with men and women who inhabit her sheltered world. **A brooding story of art and lust in the cloisters.**

Black Lace Booklist

Information is correct at time of printing. To avoid disappointment check availability before ordering. Go to www.blacklace-books.co.uk. All books are priced £6.99 unless another price is given.

☐ ARIA APPASSIONATA Juliet Hastings	ISBN 0 352 33056 2
☐ THE RELUCTANT PRINCESS Patty Glenn	ISBN 0 352 33809 1
☐ WILD IN THE COUNTRY Monica Belle	ISBN 0 352 33824 5
☐ THE TUTOR Portia Da Costa	ISBN 0 352 32946 7
☐ SEXUAL STRATEGY Felice de Vere	ISBN 0 352 33843 1
☐ HARD BLUE MIDNIGHT Alaine Hood	ISBNO 352 33851 2
☐ ALWAYS THE BRIDEGROOM Tesni Morgan	ISBNO 352 33855 5
☐ COMING ROUND THE MOUNTAIN Tabitha Flyte	ISBNO 352 33873 3

BLACK LACE BOOKS WITH AN HISTORICAL SETTING

☐ PRIMAL SKIN Leona Benkt Rhys	ISBN 0 352 33500 9 £5.99
☐ DEVIL'S FIRE Melissa MacNeal	ISBN 0 352 33527 0 £5.99
☐ DARKER THAN LOVE Kristina Lloyd	ISBN 0 352 33279 4
☐ THE CAPTIVATION Natasha Rostova	ISBN 0 352 33234 4
☐ MINX Megan Blythe	ISBN 0 352 33638 2
☐ JULIET RISING Cleo Cordell	ISBN 0 352 32938 6
☐ DEMON'S DARE Melissa MacNeal	ISBN 0 352 33683 8
☐ DIVINE TORMENT Janine Ashbless	ISBN 0 352 33719 2
☐ SATAN'S ANGEL Melissa MacNeal	ISBN 0 352 33726 5
☐ THE INTIMATE EYE Georgia Angelis	ISBN 0 352 33004 X
☐ OPAL DARKNESS Cleo Cordell	ISBN 0 352 33033 3
☐ SILKEN CHAINS Jodi Nicol	ISBN 0 352 33143 7
☐ EVIL'S NIECE Melissa MacNeal	ISBN 0 352 33781 8
☐ ACE OF HEARTS Lisette Allen	ISBN 0 352 33059 7
☐ A GENTLEMAN'S WAGER Madelynne Ellis	ISBN 0 352 33800 8
☐ THE LION LOVER Mercedes Kelly	ISBN 0 352 33162 3
☐ ARTISTIC LICENCE Vivienne La Fay	ISBN 0 352 33210 7
☐ THE AMULET Lisette Allen	ISBN 0 352 33019 8

BLACK LACE ANTHOLOGIES

☐ WICKED WORDS 6 Various	ISBN 0 352 33590 0
☐ WICKED WORDS 9 Various	ISBN 0 352 33860 1
☐ THE BEST OF BLACK LACE 2 Various	ISBN 0 352 33718 4

BLACK LACE NON-FICTION

☐ THE BLACK LACE BOOK OF WOMEN'S SEXUAL   ISBN 0 352 33793 1 £6.99
    FANTASIES Ed. Kerri Sharp

To find out the latest information about Black Lace titles, check out the website: www.blacklace-books.co.uk or send for a booklist with complete synopses by writing to:

> Black Lace Booklist, Virgin Books Ltd
> Thames Wharf Studios
> Rainville Road
> London W6 9HA

Please include an SAE of decent size. Please note only British stamps are valid.

Our privacy policy

We will not disclose information you supply us to any other parties. We will not disclose any information which identifies you personally to any person without your express consent.

From time to time we may send out information about Black Lace books and special offers. Please tick here if you do not wish to receive Black Lace information.   ☐

Please send me the books I have ticked above.

Name ....

Address ....

....

....

....

Post Code ....

Send to: Cash Sales, Black Lace Books, Thames Wharf Studios, Rainville Road, London W6 9HA.

US customers: for prices and details of how to order books for delivery by mail, call 1-800-343-4499.

Please enclose a cheque or postal order, made payable to Virgin Books Ltd, to the value of the books you have ordered plus postage and packing costs as follows:

UK and BFPO – £1.00 for the first book, 50p for each subsequent book.

Overseas (including Republic of Ireland) – £2.00 for the first book, £1.00 for each subsequent book.

If you would prefer to pay by VISA, ACCESS/MASTERCARD, DINERS CLUB, AMEX or SWITCH, please write your card number and expiry date here:

....

Signature ....

Please allow up to 28 days for delivery.